CARNAVAL

Alex Szogyi

MINERVA PRESS

LONDON

ATLANTA MONTREUX SYDNEY

CARNAVAL
Copyright © Alex Szogyi 1998

ISBN 1 86106 907 3

First Published 1998 by
MINERVA PRESS
195 Knightsbridge
London SW7 1RE

Printed in Great Britain for Minerva Press

CARNAVAL

For Gérard Depardieu, in friendship.
For Philip, as ever.

Chapter One

I remember, I remember. It was another time. It was another moment in time. It all began in class. I was teaching and getting to know yet another group of students. We were struggling through Racine's *Bérénice*. His most unusual play, the only reasonable work of passion in the seventeenth-century canon. Bérénice loved Titus and it took five acts for her to fully understand that he no longer loved her. The Jewish queen adored the Roman emperor who lost his taste for passion and life after losing his father, Vespasian. Vespasian, I told them, ever clever, is still celebrated today in Paris, since the outdoor *pissoirs* are named 'vespasiennes' in his honor. (Irony of ironies. The outdoor *pissoirs* were soon a thing of the past as mid-century made urban life more and more dangerous in big cities and the gay activities in them were soon far too perilous, indeed.) Now they have been replaced by monuments which are paid *pissoirs* and which close you off when you go into them. Very scary, because you wonder if you will ever come out, whether the door will ever open.

I free-floated about *Bérénice* and discussed love and passion in our time and then. A pair of bright eyes followed every move I made. He seemed to be half bored by it all. He looked rather like Fred McMurray, wore sloppy sweaters and kept running his long, elegant fingers through his thinning hair. His high, intelligent forehead ruminated.

He was staring at me, through me, wondering who I really was. Our eyes met frequently and one or the other of us removed ourselves from the intense mutual gaze.

Several weeks later I wandered down to one of the frats late at night for a beer and to listen to some jazz. I saw him there, playing the saxophone, lost in his music as he stared into space. I wondered whether I ought to wait and say hello after the jam session. I allowed myself to do so. He bowed, ceremoniously, half smiled.

"I didn't know you frequented these hot spots," he proffered.

"I generally do not," I answered, "but it was a balmy night and I wasn't very sleepy."

I decided to wish him a goodnight and not be too obviously present, but he had already taken the initiative.

"Are you hungry? How about some pizza?"

I acquiesced and found myself in his car, whizzing out of town to an all-night pizza place on the road. We sat watching the pizza maker give a dazzling account of himself as he twirled the dough until it took shape and then placed all the provocative toppings on it before roasting it in the oven.

"I admire that," he said. "I admire skill wherever I find it. I admire you and the way you make literature come alive."

I thanked him, awkwardly, happy that he enjoyed my teaching. We kept looking at each other on occasion and we kept avoiding each other's glances. Our eyes met momentarily each time.

"Tell me about you," I gathered up the courage to ask.

"There's nothing to tell," he played himself down. "I'm just an impassioned observer of life."

"Aren't you too young for that?"

"Never too young, never too old," he insisted.

We bantered long and hard and then I was dropped off at my house on Oak Street, where I occupied the upstairs.

"See you in class," he said as a last word before he drove off into the night.

Don (that was his name) maintained his usual provocative stance in class. I found myself more and more provocative as I discussed Racinian passion and Cornelian heroics. A few evenings later, I found him at the bottom of the stairs. He came up and we shared a beer. He wondered what I was going to be doing on the weekend. His girlfriend was coming for the weekend and he wanted to introduce her to me. Their relationship was troubling him. She was a Belgian girl named Anne. Very snazzy, very beautiful, full of pretension, a poor little rich girl. What, I wondered, was that? Oh, he said, quick to formulate and define. Poor little rich people were from very rich families but they didn't really have any money until they actually inherited. Their allowances were never enough and they invariably lived beyond their means. Sometimes they never made it to riches. Their parents lived long enough to lose all their money. But they always behaved as if they were about to be very rich.

"I'm just a simple, hard-working hick and I don't know if I deserve to have her."

"I'm sure you do," I insisted.

I wasn't going to be in town for the weekend. The big city beckoned and I would surely be in New York. He had a come-hither look in his eye.

"Could she stay in your place? I'd like to see her in a nice homey place."

"Of course," I agreed. "She can spend the weekend in my place." I would meet her at some more propitious occasion.

And so it came to pass. Don and his Anne spent weekends at my place. I would always find a token gift on return, some lovely bottle of wine, a six-pack from him or even a book about French literature, indicating how cultivated she was. She played piano, quite well, I was told, and some of her music was left on my piano. Everything seemed rehearsed. Everything seemed meant to be. He became more and more moody in class. He even missed a session or two, which disturbed me because I knew I was giving these classes for him and my comments were for his benefit. One evening, very late again, a Thursday evening, he appeared at the bottom of the stairs. He seemed disturbed, hair all tousled, a bit unkempt. He asked to come up, sat on the living room floor in front of the piano and drank a beer or two in complete silence before I tried to make him talk.

"What's bothering you?"

He looked up at me with those provocative eyes, tried to smile and then took his head in his hands. I came over to him, placed my hands on his shoulders. He wriggled away, as if I had offended him. Slowly, he said what was on his mind.

"We're in trouble."

"Trouble?" I echoed. "Tell me."

"She's pregnant."

"By you?"

"Yours truly. What am I going to do?"

"Something honorable, I hope."

"We're not going to get married."

"Why not?"

"We're not ready. That's not what I want."

"Then why did you do it?"

"I give what people want from me."

"What did she want?"

"My hot body."

"But there are precautions that can be taken."

"Yeah, yeah, we know. But hot bodies are impatient."

"What do you want me to do?"

"Maybe you could talk to her."

"I haven't even met her yet."

"Spend a weekend here and you will."

And so I allowed myself to be convinced. I was to stay for the weekend and share my adobe hacienda with Don and his lady-love. I would play parent to my two inherited children.

Anne was beautiful. Her face was a poem. Her lips were luscious and defiant. Her brown eyes were playful. Her voice was cultivated. You could see what attracted her to Don but they were the same age and she needed an older, more sophisticated man. As soon as we were all ensconced in the living room with our drinks in hand, Don used a pretext to abscond. He would be back in a few hours, time for us to get to know each other a little.

We both looked after him, dreading what the next few hours would be like. I tried to be friendly and urbane. I asked her all about herself. She had come recently from Belgium. Her parents were well off, separated, cold as ice. Her mother despised her daughter. Her father loved her but was constantly testing her. She was an only child, musical; played the piano rather well and was contemplating a concert career if she could get it together. Don was a mistake. She came right out and said so. She was attracted to him but he was far too tentative and deeply

confused, as she put it. Rotten luck to be pregnant so soon.
They could have been friends. Now they had to break it off
so soon. Oh, she liked him and she thought he was a sweet
fellow, but she couldn't have his child. She didn't really
want an abortion, but who would bring up their child? If
only she could give the child to someone. Don and she
didn't really want it. She began to cry, ever so slightly,
walked over to me and threw herself in my arms. I felt such
compassion for her and not a little desire, as if she knew I
was right for her. I let her stay in the crook of my arm until
it seemed an eternity. I thought she was going to ask me to
make love to her and part of me wanted it. Perhaps, some
day. Some other day.

"You're very kind. I knew you would be. Don told me
what a lovely man you were. I couldn't wait to meet you."
She thrust her petulant lips towards me. I wanted to bite
them and I just stood there and smiled.

"What can I do for you... both?" I asked, not knowing
what I meant.

"Help us. Be with us. Counsel us. Help us to make up
our minds."

Don appeared. He sensed that we had gotten to know
one another rather quickly. He was relieved. His usual
bravado came back. He made us more drinks and we sat
there drinking until we were all three rather high. Then we
went off to dinner. Anne and I discussed French literature
and music. Don sat there and drank it in.

When dinner was over, we returned to the apartment. I
gave the two of them my room at the end of the hall. I
decided to sleep on the living room couch. He came in to
say goodnight to me, hovered over my bed, tucked the
sheets in a bit and whispered: "Thanks. I'll never forget
you."

Later I went to the bathroom in the hallway before deciding to fall asleep for the night. As I came out, I saw her there in front of the door. She fell into my arms, kissed me rather tentatively on the mouth and let me brush past her without a word. I was so excited by it all that I was up half the night, tossing and turning.

In the morning I decided to go off to New York for the rest of the weekend. I was visibly shaken and they seemed to understand my state. They didn't try to stop me. They seemed to be enjoying their own company. They must have made love again during the night.

When I returned on Sunday evening, they had left. The beds were made. The refrigerator was pleasantly stocked. There was a note from Anne. I sat and read it quietly. 'You are a prince. We love you. We will behave. Have patience with us. Until soon.' It was signed by her, not him.

A sound came up towards me from the bottom of the stairs. It was Don. I was relieved. My heart beat faster as he came up the stairs, ever surly, ever troubled. He poured himself a beer.

"Tell me," I said, ever impatient.

"You helped us. I knew she needed to meet you. She told me she wished she had fallen in love with you. I may just start being jealous of you."

"Please don't. She naturally likes older men."

"She likes any man. A cock and balls. That's all she needs to be inspired."

"Now, down boy. That's unkind."

"Unkind, but true."

"She's a beautiful girl. She doesn't yet understand herself."

"And you're there to help her understand herself, right?"

He took his fist and made me believe he was about to hit me on the chin.

"I wouldn't blame you," I said. "But I didn't start this."

"You can have her. I don't want her any more."

"What are you going to do with the baby?"

"She's going to have an abortion. I'll pay for it."

"Are you sure that's the best thing? I don't like abortions. They're dangerous."

"Well, you can marry her and bring up our child. I'll come for weekend visits."

"Don't be snide. I'm willing to help you both, but I won't stand for your being nasty."

"She told me you were the sort of man she would like."

"I really don't believe that for a minute. She's troubled."

He sat down on the floor in front of the piano, his favorite place to be. He rose to get me a beer and he opened one for himself. We sat there for the longest time, not saying anything, breathing in each other's presence. I felt just as confused as he did.

"Where is she?" I finally asked, afraid she might be somewhere near.

"She said she was going home for a while to think. She was going to see her father."

"Not her mother?"

"Her mother would kill her. Her mother would force her to marry me or somebody else."

"We all need a little time to think."

Don decided to put on a favorite record of his. We both liked it. Background music for Marlon Brando movies. We used to listen to it a great deal and now it seemed to sum up our feelings.

Then he turned and walked straight to the fridge.

"Gin and tonic?" I asked, alive to his every movement.

"Yeah. Keep the old malaria down."

He pried out the ice tray and knocked it against the sink briefly to shake the cubes free.

"Coldest ice cubes in the world. Cold as a witch's teat."

"There's some cheese and crackers, too. We mustn't get too high on all this."

Now ritualized, affable and adjoined in the rhythm of the ritual, we had created our own indelible atmosphere.

He splashed out the equivalent of about four jiggers into each glass. The quinine water fizzed to the top and overflowed generously on to the Formica. He fumbled with records, choosing the Brando.

I tried not to watch his backs and forths too intently. He kicked off his shoes. He took out a pack of cigarettes and threw one at me absently, lit it for me, took a huge gulp of his drink, and announced, as part of the ritual: "I feel like getting blasted," and, for effect, "blasted out of my fucking mind."

We settled back into our respective positions. His nervous fingers strummed on the edge of his glass.

He threw his sweater on the back of his chair and it hung there like a limp effigy of himself.

"I like the way you throw your clothes around."

"The way I throw everything around. Listen to that. They know how to play."

I stared at him. I allowed myself to scrutinize, memorize him for later, for the inevitable moments when he wouldn't be there for me to contemplate. Every move was indelible. Such grace welded to such self-consciousness. Our eyes met. He looked at me. Strong and hard.

There was meanness in the glance, more than I would acknowledge.

"You poor bastard."

"What do you mean?"

"You know what I mean."

"No, I don't."

"You really feel something."

"Now stop that."

"Stop what?"

"Stop trying to humiliate me."

"Can it." A pause. "Oh well, what the hell."

He threw off his pants and underwear with the quick bravado which had liberated the ice cubes.

"It's hot in here. Why don't you take your clothes off too?"

I followed suit, more slowly, more deliberately. The liquor had taken effect. We both gulped it more and more. He turned up the music to a blast. I tried not to look at him any more. I knew he was coming toward me, contemplating me. He came and stood close to me, innocence coupled with intense knowledge. I looked past him to the cold purity of the gin bottle.

He laughed earthily. "Now you're going to have to be very kind. Because I have no experience with any of this."

His genitals jiggled forth in the half-light, high and hot. The music blared. He thrust himself towards me. The ritual had begun.

We exhausted ourselves in the wildest lovemaking I had ever known. He tried to be gentle and found himself the aggressor. He took me down the hallway to the bedroom and threw me on the bed. He mounted me and penetrated me with intense agility. We lay there exhausted and breathing deeply.

"Now are you happy?" I asked.

"Now you know what she feels, what she wanted. Cock and balls."

"But there's more to it than that," I suggested.

"Much more," he conceded. "Only you won't get pregnant."

"You know this is only the beginning," I continued.

"Or the end."

I started kissing him slowly on the mouth. He became erect again and substituted his aching groin for his mouth. As I worked him, I heard him whisper ecstatically, "Oh, sweetheart. Oh sweetheart, oh..."

We were enveloped in the music and the moment and I knew that we had begun an experiment we would have to have the courage to pursue. Between us was Anne, her presence muted, her desire our inspiration.

Chapter Two

Excitement was rampant on campus. The great soprano, Mariana Herzlich, was to grace the college with her presence. It was a new caper of the music department. Invite great artists to perform there before their recitals in New York. The exquisite Mariana was the first.

Things could get very morose on campus. A few bad days, a spate of dismal weather, endemic boredom, all led to a feeling that nothing would ever get better. Tolstoy called Paris the tomb of the world. And if beauteous Paris could become an abyss, so could Middletown. Don had not been in class this day. He was off to New York to meet Anne's redoubtable parents. She had confessed and the much needed abortion was performed. Don insisted on facing the music and on paying the price. I felt part of it all and had to keep reminding myself I wasn't.

To distract myself, I went off to Helmut and Elizabeth's, the best place on campus for unrelenting gossip and civilized atmosphere. At tea time, the best of the campus were there, elegant cups in hand, ever ready to create high-class gossip in a high-class ambiance. That was what I needed, the artificiality of the moment. I never felt part of it all, but they were willing to include me in their midst. Perhaps something I did in New York would be worthy and then they would feel that I was, indeed, worth the attention. Besides, I was part of a new production of

Chekhov's *The Cherry Orchard* at the '92 Theater, where the most daring theater productions were forever burgeoning. This was the baby of Ralph Porter, Mr. Preciosity himself. Imagine doing *The Cherry Orchard* with no décor. Perhaps the most decorous of all plays in the history of theater could only succeed without décor if the acting was of the absolute finest. The cast, all things considered, was rather talented. I played Gayev, the wayward brother and I understood the Chekhovian motivations.

As I meandered over to Helmut and Elizabeth's, I realized anew that life was no longer the same since I had met Don and his Anne. I was part of a new sensual world I could never have hoped for and it was so intense that I could barely do anything else between bouts. I needed this tea party to put my life into perspective. They would all faint dead away if they knew what I was involved with, but it was probable that their lives were not so very innocent, either. Rumors hung heavy. Nearly all the marriages on campus had had rumors of wild hanky panky and it was the theory of Paul Barlow, the novelist, that no relationship was ever safe in this den of iniquity. He had often told me to escape. I was young enough, I wasn't married and I had a life in New York. It was better not to remain. Almost everyone was broken sooner or later, every relationship a prey to the insidious boredom which took over after a while.

Elizabeth answered the door bell, smiled her Hungarian smile, ever more Austrian due to her long relationship with her husband. The Hungarians and the Austrians were of the same empire but not of the same world. The Hungarians were strong, wily, willful. The Viennese were culturally superior, false as their whipped cream, *schlag*, and we were always reminded that it was in Austria that Hitler came to power. Still, it was a perfect marriage. Helmut was the former curator of one of the major small museums of Vienna and knew everything there was to know about everything in the world of art. He looked down at us all as if we were lackeys of some sort. His mission was to educate us. Elizabeth's mission was to keep him intact. She was also a dancing teacher and she took those on campus with no real flair for body development and shaped their sagging torsos. She had a wonderful Hungarian laugh. Being with them was endlessly amusing. Helmut had promised us that he would find art works for us that we could afford, the right names, the right prices which would one day be worth *something*. We were to have our little masterpieces delivered that day. There was a sense of hushed excitement.

Barlow was ensconced in the largest armchair. He was everyone's guru. The entire campus worshipped his brilliance. He had written several novels and published them. Then he lost one. He had mailed it to his publisher without making a copy and it had never arrived. He was slightly embittered by the contretemps.

"Here comes our Off-Broadway translator," said he, announcing me. "I see you have time for us today."

"Bitch, bitch," came a sexy voice nearby.

It was Dana, the campus whore, married to colleague Harry. She was young and sexy and everybody had their Dana story. She had her macabre side, besides her penchant for sleeping with everything that moved. She had a tarantula in her living room (under glass), but since tarantulas shed their skin every year, she kept the skin on the coffee table, relishing the fright it raised in almost all her guests. Dana's favorite pastime was shelling and deveining shrimp. Whenever I had a dinner party, I invited her to do the dirty work and she always thanked me. We embraced and I forbid myself to see if she would play a practical joke, which she was prone to do. I loved her being there. She always cut other people's nonsense with her macabre behavior. Harry was there, as well, ever saccharin sweet, a gentleman who must have driven Dana mad with his gentlemanly ways. One always wondered why certain people ever bothered to get married. It was perhaps a trick of destiny or a karmic punishment. It always had to be worked out.

There was also Johann. Sexy, manly Johann, the German professor. He was a charming man and it took a long time to discover that he was only interested in you if you had money, power or position. Married wives always fell for him. He was never available, really, because he had a young male lover, still a student, but he fooled them all.

They didn't live happily ever after but they were always together. Both rather Germanic, they had probably come together to punish one another. I got to know Johann rather well after a while and he would tell me about his difficult bonding. They would lie close together and rub up against each other until they ejaculated. How much easier it was to be heterosexual. There were certain things you did and although the missionary position was rather rare, there were at least the things one could call expected or normal. Sexuality between men was more inventive, more unpredictable, although it was possible for one man to treat the other like a woman, take the missionary position, and create a false vagina for the occasion. That almost made them man and woman. All things were possible.

Sam and Beulah were there, too. They were a sensationally beautiful couple. He was the head of the art museum and a painter in his own right. There were rampant stories about his affairs with male students but when he was with his wife, one could not believe them. She was sweetness itself, always a young lady but with a mind so brilliant that it was impossible to believe her beauty. She had everything. And, unlike most of the other wives on campus, she had eyes only for her splendid husband. Fidelity always fascinated me. Perhaps some people were born for it. It certainly didn't mean a lack of temperament. It was a beatific state, as if one had been given one's life partner and one accepted it. Paradise on earth. Love forever. It could happen, even on this campus. Even with a brood of children and every distraction possible.

There they all were, the choice characters of the moment. Helmut proceeded to bring out the art works. Everyone applauded the splendid drawings and etchings, minor works by the major masters, given to us for a song. I received a Matisse drawing of a woman's head all done in one pencil line, a miraculous creation which seemed worthy of a king's ransom. Then there was a page from a Spanish book illustrated by the redoubtable Picasso. It was full of black and red panache. And then there was a young *saltimbanque*, a dancer by Rouault, unmistakably of this style. And finally, a delicious Daumier, of a portly gentleman trying to digest a huge meal. There was a huge pear resting on his fat abdomen, mimicking the feeling one has after overeating. Could I ever live without that in the future? Certainly not. Helmut was proud of himself. Everyone applauded. For a moment I forgot Don and his Anne and I was just an art collector in the presence of his intellectual peers.

I embraced Helmut. He basked in the attention and I will always remember that lovely proprietary moment. Each of us rejoiced in the others' new possessions. Dana seemed a bit bored. There was nothing for her and neither was there any young man to be attracted to except Johann. And she knew she couldn't really have him. She found the way to leave. Within a half hour, everyone had dispersed and I realized I, too, had to go back home and figure out what to do for the evening.

I went back, climbed the stairs wearily and sat down in the living room. I put the Brando record on and sat there with a beer. Don was in my mind. His body was indelibly in my body and I kept thinking where all this might lead. I had to put him out of my mind. I had to start living the way I had. I had always been alone, a loner. I had never allowed myself to live with anyone or to have a relationship because I didn't want my parents to find out. In those days, we weren't worried about disease or death. We were afraid of detection. We had to live a quiet life because our reputations might be ruined. We had to create our own myth, talk about our lives, or else everyone would make up a story which wasn't true. I could even make up a plausible story now. The girlfriend of my favorite student had fallen for me. What was I to do? I would try not to ruin her life. I would try to help her to become a happier, wiser person. I would try to understand what she wanted. But what of Don? What did he want? How could I help him? How could I keep from drowning in his masculinity, in his willfulness? How could I make him happy and myself as well? How could I forget him from time to time? Why was I so obsessed with him? Why did I care so much? What did he have that I needed? How could I define it for myself? For him? What did it all mean?

I heard footsteps outside. Could it be Don? I drank my beer down before I investigated. The doorbell rang. That wasn't like him. He didn't like to ring. I looked out the window glass at the door and saw Peter. Peter, my worst student, a magnificent goof off. Why was I so nice to him? I invariably had good relationships with my worst students. Peter should never have gone to college. He certainly had no flair for languages. I had offered to help him. He had taken me up on it but recently he had simply kept on goofing off.

"Peter. To what do I owe this honor?"

"Hi, teach. I was passing by and I thought of saying hello."

"What did you have in mind?"

"I really have to pass that course of yours. And I don't see how I will. So I thought I'd offer to pay you for extra lessons, if you know what I mean." Peter's arch smile decorated his face and made him look like a hustler.

"I'm already paid for that service, Peter. I have it as my duty to help you. But only if you want to be helped."

"I'm not really sure you can help me. But I'd be glad to pay for a passing grade. I'd do just about anything, if you know what I mean."

"I don't know what you mean, Peter, but you'll only get a decent grade if you get a good mark on the final. So let's not do anything louche here. Okay?"

"Sure, teach. Sure. I just wanted you to know that I think you're a great guy and I wish I were as good in French as I am in football. We can't all be perfect in everything, you know."

"That's true, my good man. But Peter, you have got to knuckle under and start doing a little work."

He nodded, serious and convinced. "I've got a new girl and she's really something. You'd love her. Her father is a college president, worse luck. So that if I don't do well or can't get through, there's just no way she's ever going to take me seriously. You see?"

I nodded, realizing the real reason for the evening visit. "You mean you're serious about this young lady and she wants you to be a decent student. Or else her father does."

"That's it. I have no luck. The fact that I'm superior at football or a jock doesn't mean a thing to them. They all speak French. I can't fail this course. I just can't."

"Why don't you let her teach you French, Peter? They say that if you study with a loved one, the motivation gets the work accomplished."

"Didn't you ever hear the story about it being impossible to learn how to drive if the teacher is close to you?"

"Yes, but, learning to drive and learning French is not quite the same thing, is it?"

"Well, why not? Both have rules and ways of doing it."

"You have a point."

"So, help me." He sat down and looked at me, almost groveling, genuinely concerned this time.

I laughed. "Very well, Peter, we'll start really studying for this final exam. And you're going to get through."

He jumped up, put his arm around me, fraternally, and smiled his insidious smile. "You're a great guy. I'll make it worth your while. I'll give you something you'll never forget."

"Just don't tell me what that is."

The door opened without a warning. It was Don, with a mean scowl on his face. He said, insidiously: "Am I interrupting?"

Peter and I looked as if we had been doing something wrong when we actually hadn't. Peter took the initiative: "Hi, Don, how are you, fella? You look a little under the weather."

No answer was forthcoming. Peter realized somehow that he was de trop and left immediately. "Thanks, teach. I'll remember your advice. *Mille grazie.*"

I pointed to the couch. Don went over and sat down, still scowling. He threw off his sweater. "I see I'm not the only one in your life these days."

"Shut up. Don't you have any standards? That's poor Peter. He has to pass the course and he's desperate."

"Well, you know how to solve that."

"If you don't behave, I'm going to ask you to leave."

"Don't, please. I have to talk to you."

"How is Anne? Did you meet her father?"

"Father and mother both. The deed is done."

"How is she?"

"Just fine. She's a hardy soul."

"Did you have to pay?"

"I offered but they wouldn't have it. They just asked me to leave her alone in the future."

"Will you?"

"Sure. After all, now I have a boyfriend. That's absorbing enough."

"You don't have a boy friend", I said emphatically. "You have an Anne substitute."

"I'm thorough and when I start something, I finish it."

"Well then, finish it. I don't want to suffer your bad temper."

He got up and came over to me, pulling me into him. He was crying. "You know, I'm still very young. I can get hurt. I don't know what I'm doing. Up till now, I've trusted you. I hero worship you. You're my guru. You're my role model. You're my..."

"Lover," I suggested.

"I don't know what that means. But when I'm close to you, you make me want you. But I told you to be kind."

I was deeply touched. I changed my attitude instantly.

"Don, you know I care about you. But I don't want to start something with you if you hurt me or leave me right away. I'm afraid. This is just as difficult for me as it is for you."

He took my hand, drew me down the hall to the bedroom. We sat down on the bed and stared at each other. Who would make the first move? Where would it lead?

I caressed his cheek with my right hand. The tears fell from his eyes and he held ferociously on to me, sobbing uncontrollably. He lay back on the bed, as if crucified, as if mortified. I sat looking at him, at the most beautiful man I had ever contemplated. Finally, I lay my head on his stomach and we fell asleep as purely as two babes in the wood. When we awakened hours later, his hungry lips searched for mine and we merged in unthought of bliss.

Chapter Three

Over breakfast, I showed him my new acquisitions. Don looked at them critically.

"I hope they're not cheating you."

"I never thought of that. What do you know about art?"

"Only through what I create myself."

"You?"

He smiled, knowingly. "I paint."

"That's exciting. Why didn't you tell me?"

"We reveal things slowly in my family. When Anne wasn't here, I used to spend my weekends painting."

"Where?"

"I have a studio on campus. I'll invite you over. But I used to use it to get away from people and things."

"I'll be over. Whenever you say."

"It's a date."

"What are you doing today?"

"We've been called over to the music department. There's a concert tonight."

"Oh, yes, Mariana Herzlich. The great German soprano."

"We're going to have to squire her around."

"What fun. I'll be at the concert, as most everyone will."

"Culture vultures."

"Maybe you can come over after the concert. I'd love to see you."

"I'll see."

The phone rang. I answered it perfunctorily. It was Anne's voice at the other end. I stiffened.

"Anne? How are you. Don told me you went through with it."

"I'm fine. I'll live. A little post-partum triste. Who knows, it might have been a very special child."

"Surely."

"I'd like to ask you for a favor. I can't wait to get away from my parents. Could I come up and visit you for the weekend? I promise I'll be good."

"If you'd like. Don will be here." I looked at Don. He was sitting there, ready to pounce. "In fact..."

Don waved to me not to say he was there. He placed his fingers on his lips.

Anne continued: "I'd like to recuperate with you. Please don't tell him I'm coming."

"I'll try not to. But he might drop over."

"*Que será, será.* But I've got to get out of here. I'll be up on Friday evening. Expect me for supper."

"Take good care of yourself."

"Ciao."

I set down the receiver and stared at Don.

"I told you she wanted you."

"That's not true. She wants to hide. I have the place to do that."

"And she wants me out of it all."

"That's not my agenda. Just give me an evening with her. I'll have the two of you back knowing each other. No fear."

"I think she might be right. I may spend the weekend in painting isolation."

"Let's not think about it. Sufficient unto the day. I'll see you after the concert. One event at a time."

He got up, as if he were anxious to leave. He wasn't dressed. We were both in the altogether. I didn't want to let him go. He came towards me and kissed me on the forehead.

"I'll see you later."

"Don't go just yet, please."

We went down the corridor into the bedroom and held each other for another moment. We made love once again, as if we couldn't bear to separate. I was too exhausted to move. He dressed and, as he left, he looked most seriously at me. "You can pose for me any time you like."

"Not in the altogether."

"I doubt it."

"Don't worry."

"Don't leave me for her."

"No chance."

"See you later, lover."

He waved goodbye and I heard him go down the stairs.

Chapter Four

Mariana Herzlich was there. The redoubtable soprano attracted the elite of the campus. They were all there ready to judge her. Could she be as good as her records? Wasn't she already over the hill? We would soon know. I walked into the back of the concert hall and saw all my friends. I didn't want any of their customary bitchiness. I wanted to sit next to someone compassionate who had come to be wafted through the music. It didn't matter what she sang like. I wanted the oblivion only music can bring.

I saw Carolyn sitting by herself. The most entertaining person on campus. She was always bright-eyed and bushy-tailed. She had made a bad marriage and was always making the best of it. Her husband and she stuck together, despite the impossibility of their relationship. She recounted marvelous tales of her wedding day. Both of them sat in the car and each of them threw up on the way to the ceremony, each from a different window. They had two daughters and never appeared in the same places, for parties, occasions or whatnot. She, too, was in *The Cherry Orchard*. If she rehearsed enough, she would not have to see him very much for that period. They still made believe they weren't avoiding one another. I slid down next to her.

"Hello. I was hoping you'd be here."

"It's mutual."

"Have you ever heard her sing?"

"I have hundreds of her records. She's my favorite soprano."

"I don't trust her because she's German. But I suppose the voice has nothing to do with the nationality."

"We'll discuss that later. Meanwhile, let's case the joint."

We stared at the gathering. A moment later, the beauteous soprano arrived, dressed in bright red silk. I would see her many times in the years to come. She always chose a different color and different style. She never sang the same program twice. But her encores were inevitably the same and years later even Monserrat Caballé would make fun of her choice of a certain Swiss folksong, as an encore. She basked in the audience's worship, smiled benevolently and indicated to her subservient pianist that it was time to start. It was a moment before I noticed the page turner. He was tall and handsome and... I suddenly realized who it was. It was Don, surely it was he. He had kept this for a surprise. The man was full of surprises. I could see him enjoying my reaction later this evening. Was it Don? No matter what he wore, he looked completely different. He was minus his ratty sweater. His hair was combed back, even slicked. I could only think of him in class and then naked and vulnerable. What if he had appeared naked on stage for his subservient role in the musical proceedings? Even Mariana Herzlich could not have survived that.

Carolyn looked strangely at me. "You seem distracted, my dear."

"It's nothing," I said. "The world is too much with me."

"Now sit back and listen. Be a good boy."

Chapter Five

Encores followed encores and it was a notable triumph. Helmut and Elizabeth were particularly proud. They passed us with their contingent on the way out. "Distinguished", was a word heard here and there.

"She certainly knows how to dress," Barlow was heard to proffer.

Carolyn and I went out for coffee with Beatrice and Aram, two of the most personable members of the campus. He was a distinguished professor of comparative literature, she a delightful woman of the Netherlands, quiet, loving and deeply enigmatic. They would soon divorce but they were staying together for the sake of their son. Carolyn's effervescence was all we needed to make a happy foursome.

"Where is Bill?" she was asked.

"Oh, marking papers late or doing something useful. He doesn't have time for art and culture, unless he's out to prove something."

Coffee was pleasant and we had a liqueur as well, in Middletown's German restaurant, Goldwasser, full of little gold leaves. We toasted the great lady of song in her absence.

"She's going to be at the music department tomorrow afternoon," Beatrice informed us. "Only the lucky few will be invited to have a drink with her."

They had been invited, I was not. I would see about that with Don, later, to see if he was on duty. Then I could sneak in.

Carolyn was always sure of herself: "Oh, just show up. Nobody ever remembers who's invited and who's not. I intend to go. I'll speak German with her. That will do it."

By the time I returned to Oak Street, I was afraid Don might have come and gone. But I was damned if I would cut short every moment just to be with him. I had to have some dignity. He was sitting on the stairs waiting for me.

"Baying at the moon, I see. It must have been exciting being the page turner."

"I didn't know I would be chosen. But somebody heard that I played a musical instrument. They needed someone who could read music."

"So many talents. What are you going to do with your life? Will you be an artist, a musician, a painter? What will it be?"

"Who knows? I think I'll end up doing something rather mundane."

"We'll have to discuss it. I understand that the great lady will be fêted at tea tomorrow. Will you be there?"

Don hesitated. "Yes, I have to be in service. I'll have to distribute the beer and pretzels."

"Beer and pretzels!" I gasped.

"Well, you know the music department. They're so chintzy."

"You can't serve beer and pretzels to the high priestess of song. That would be sacrilege. Doesn't anyone have a little funds for champagne?"

"Not everybody lives as high on the hog as our French professor."

"It's a matter of taste. You don't serve a great diva beer and pretzels, even if she is German."

"What's to say she doesn't like beer?"

"Well, maybe she does, but you should give her the option of something more elegant."

"They'll do it up proud. Don't worry. She does have a beautiful voice, doesn't she, and the greatest diction."

"I've never heard anything like it. She's positively regal."

"I was bored silly."

"Why? After all, you were on the qui vive. You had to be sure of each moment."

"That's not hard to do. But I would like to have been listening to it with you."

"Come to think of it, so would I."

"Do you have any of her records?"

"As a matter of fact, I do. What would you like to hear?"

"Something simple. Quiet. Peaceful."

"I have some Mozart songs."

"Put them on."

I found them behind some other records and did so. "And may I serve you some champagne, my young fellow?"

"Let's save that for an occasion. I'll have the usual beer."

"Ever the plebeian".

"Don't forget I'm from the middle west."

We sat listening to the pure tones of Mariana Herzlich. There was peace in the air. Don drank in the soprano tones and slowly merged into the sound. We were infinitely quiet, light headed and as happy as we had been for the last day or so. After a while, he rose, put down his glass and bowed to me, very formal. "I bid you a goodnight."

I couldn't bear his leaving. "Won't you do me the honor of spending the night?"

"If you insist. Does she sing any waltzes?"

"I think I have some."

"Please put them on, sir."

I searched for some *Rosenkavalier*. I put it on. He came over and beckoned me to dance. We waltzed around somewhat awkwardly, laughing a bit. Then he took me in his arms and waltzed me down the corridor.

Another glorious moment began.

Chapter Six

The music department was honoring Mariana Herzlich. She was very beautiful and very out of her element. People stopped to congratulate her. I nearly had a fit when someone actually offered her beer and pretzels. She declined, most politely. I ran over to ask her what she would like to have? Champagne? Though I feared that if she said yes, it would take me too long to get home and back with a bottle of Veuve Cliquot.

"I should like a cup of tea, if there is any."

"Of course," I said, and ran to the kitchen. There I commandeered a pot of tea and asked Don to bring it. Meanwhile, I returned to sit near her and fend questions, should they be embarrassing.

We discussed her coming first to the sticks and then to New York.

"It's most amusing", she said "to see how a little university town functions. I might very well prefer it to the big city."

Did she have friends in New York? Professional acquaintances, of course and her husband was due soon to join her. For the moment, she wished to breathe in the atmosphere of the new world. She was so gracious that I was at a loss to know what to say. It was more difficult with Mme Herzlich because she was less candid. When Don brought her tea, she beckoned him to sit next to her and questioned him about his love for music. He was painfully shy but did better than I did in my enthusiasm. I didn't wish her to know that we were connected and so I held back even more.

"If you love music, you must pursue it. You must be serious in your studies because one never has a moment to lose. And you seem very serious, indeed, young man."

She was asked to another fraternity for a cocktail and so she was ready to be on her way as soon as the last drop of the tea was consumed. I offered to drive her to the fraternity. Fortunately, Don had his car out front and so we did the honors together. This second social moment was much more successful. She had a glass of wine and seemed to be enjoying several of her conversations. The hors d'oeuvre even seemed civilized. Carolyn was there and seeing us surrounding her, she gave me a 'V' for victory symbol quite subtly, that only I could see. Harry and Dana were staring at me with noticeable jealousy and pique. I knew I'd get a phone call from one or the other of them within the next day or so. When the time came for Mme Herzlich to leave, it was obvious she no longer needed us. Her Cadillac had arrived from New York and she was escorted to it with a good dozen people in tow. One of the fraternity members tried his luck: "Won't you have breakfast tomorrow morning at the frat?"

She smiled knowingly and, as she lowered herself luxuriously into her back seat, waving to the applauding, admiring hordes, said: "Life is too short to spend two nights in Middletown."

I often quoted her changing it to: "Life is too short to spend vun night in Meedletown," enlarging on the accent. It would become my theme song and I would keep repeating it until I myself found the way to go to live in New York definitively.

Don and I drove back to the house. We walked upstairs in a state of elation, although he was somewhat moody. "Herzlich?"

"No thanks. How about some hot jazz. Or cool jazz."

"Your wish is my command."

We sat there and drank it in, punctuated with more and more beers.

"Thank you," I said. "You've given me a wonderful time. I'll never forget any of this."

"You better not." Then he became intensely quiet.

Finally I broke the silence: "What's the matter?"

"Tomorrow's Friday. She's arriving."

"Oh yes." I had been trying to forget it. "Right you are."

"I'll stay out of your way. She obviously wants to be alone with you."

"Where will you be found?"

"I'll be painting."

"Can I come get you?"

"Yes, but don't bring her."

"Don't you want to see her?"

"Yes... and no."

"We can have a civilized dinner together."

"Only if she says okay."

"I have some say in this. She's my guest, after all."

"How long will she stay?"

"We didn't discuss it."

"Life is too short to spend two nights in Middletown," he said, mocking me.

"That depends on with who..."

"With whom."

"You're a stickler."

"When it comes to you, I am."

"We won't neglect you. You're part of all this. I'm just the catalyst."

"You're the poppa pussy and she's the cunt."

"You always find the way to make things look worse than they are."

"It's my nature. I can't let well enough alone."

"Then let it alone. Don't make me angry."

"Don't make me angry. Make me happy."

"That's all I want to do. That's all I care about."

"Then shut up and let's just be together."

"Don, baby, behave."

He got up and went towards the door. I ran after him, of course and barred the door. He pushed me away and walked slowly down the steps.

I yelled after him. "Don't do this. Don't ruin everything."

He walked off. I was in a fury. Every time I thought everything would be all right, everything turned bad. There was something in him that wanted too much and then renounced too easily. I had to understand him and I didn't. But I was determined not to suffer. I had to handle her tomorrow and I wouldn't allow myself to be in a state for her arrival. I went down the corridor by myself, undressed in the dark and lay there in a fury. A storm began and thunder and lightning were the obbligato of the night.

I couldn't sleep. It was no use. Suddenly, I thought I heard someone coming. I tried to prevent myself from going to verify. I looked through the door. It was pouring and Don was at the foot of the stairs. He was urinating into the night. More bravado. I opened the door and beckoned him. He hurtled up the stairs, wildly drunk.

"Who do you think you are, Marlon Brando?"

"Screw you."

"If you wish."

He allowed me to pull him up.

He allowed me to get him through the door. He made me all wet and I managed to get his clothes off. He had the forlorn look of a Caravaggio nude. I dragged him down the corridor into bed. I tried to make love to him and he turned away.

"What's the matter with you?"

"You know why I come here."

"No. Tell me."

"To get my rocks off." He turned me over and brutally made love to me. We both cried until we came shamelessly all over the place.

Chapter Seven

Anne sat comfortably on the couch. She was buffing her nails, every inch the Jewish princess. Her ineffably lovely face seemed calm and collected. I sat watching her and wondering where the conversation would go. She didn't seem to wish it to go anywhere in particular. I sent out a trial balloon.

"How are you?"

"I'm not sure. I feel as if I have been through something very important but I'm not sure what it is."

"Try and tell me."

"I'm so very happy to be here with you."

"Why?"

"You calm me. I feel that you are not judgmental with me... or anyone. You're such a kind person."

"I wish that were true."

"You've been so good to Don and to me."

"That's a pleasure."

"What do you think of Don?"

"That was something I was going to ask of you."

She looked up at me. "Well then, let's trade impressions of him. That will help us to get acquainted."

"How did you meet?"

"I was invited up here by a friend and we met late one evening at a party. How did you meet him?"

"He was sitting in one of my classes in French literature. We were studying Racine's *Bérénice*."

"Did he enjoy it? Did he even read it?"

"I think he did. He certainly enjoyed the class. Then we met the same way you did. He was playing music late one night and I happened by."

"He seems to be more human when he is in connection somehow with the arts."

"He was the page turner for Mariana Herzlich this last week."

"Imagine that. Isn't she marvelous? I worship her interpretations."

"I do, too."

"I knew we had everything in common."

"We have had a similar education. What do you intend to do with your life?"

"I'm not sure yet. I'll either marry very rich. Or become a pianist. Or a photographer. Or even a composer."

"Why not all of these things?"

"I wouldn't mind. I want to have a very active life. And I want to make love in the finest way possible."

"Did you enjoy making love to Don?"

"Oh, yes. He is incredibly sensitive. A wonderful lover. Though every once in a while I had the impression that he wasn't really with it. He has a corner of him... which is, how shall I say it, anthropomorphic. He's a man but he's also intensely feminine. When he slept with me, I kept feeling he was observing me, wanting to be in my skin, finding out what it was to be me."

"Very well observed. There is a double side to his nature, I do believe."

"Do you think he's bisexual? When he's around you, I feel that he would be even more attracted to you than to me, or any other girl."

"Really?"

"You have to watch him."

"That's what I've been doing."

"I think he's worth it."

"A diamond in the rough?"

"A diamond in the buff. I don't want to hurt him."

"He doesn't wish to hurt you, either."

"Did he say so? I think about him a great deal. But I know there's no future for us. I need a mature man. Someone who already has status."

"Most girls your age with special talents would certainly feel that way."

"I came to ask for your help."

"What can I do for you?"

"Help me to calm him. I'm afraid he may hate me."

"He has a tendency to exaggerate emotionally. But I think he's just as afraid of you as you are of him."

"I want him to be happy. I want him to find the person who will help him to be happy. That isn't so easy to come by. Perhaps you could guide him to a happier existence."

"That's what I'm trying to do."

"But can he do it without making love? He seems to bond with someone only if he sleeps with them."

"Well then he has to learn that sex and love and companionship are not necessarily united in one person."

"How well you say that. I hope you're wrong."

"So do I."

We both laughed. She was in a chipper mood. "Shall I play something for you?"

"I would enjoy that."

"Let me play some of the sequences from Schumann's *Carnaval*. It's a divine piece. I'm working it up now for a recital. It's a genius of a piece. It ends, you know, with a great march of the professors, an academic profession, ideal for a college."

"Perhaps you might play it here sometime. We love inviting people to play."

"Oh, but I'm not known at all."

"That doesn't matter. We could do it of an evening here. I'll make a dinner in your honor."

She sat down and played a bit of *Carnaval*. It was full of brio and vivaciousness. Early Schumann was ecstatically beautiful. Melodic, full of harmonic echoes, the essence of the Romantic period. There was even one sequence that was more purely Chopinesque than Chopin.

"You play exquisitely, Anne. You must pursue this part of your talent."

"I will, for a while. I know myself. I'm infinitely distractible. If I were your mistress, I'd do just that."

I remained silent.

"But I know I never could be. You wouldn't want me for long. And Don would hate me if I monopolized you."

"How do you know that?"

"He's fiercely jealous. He'd do something outlandish."

"Well then, we better behave."

"I'd like to take you out to dinner. Somewhere quiet. You deserve everything."

"I shall be doing the taking."

"No, you won't. Don't forget, I'm the poor little rich girl. That's what Don calls me. And, you know, he's right."

We went out to avoid being alone with each other. Both of us wished to do the right thing.

It was a wonderfully enjoyable dinner. We had champagne to celebrate the event. Anne regaled me with tales of marvelous dinners she had had here and in Belgium. She told me about her fabulous parents, her adventures. Don was not her first, nor would he be her last. She was ready for married life, children, a career. She was at a turning point of her existence. Life was about to take hold of her and take her to a major moment. Don and the pregnancy were but an interlude. I kept wondering whether he was just an interlude for me. Sometimes I felt that there would be no one after him. He would take hold of me, master me and then I would never be available for anyone else. Did she understand all of that implicitly? Was she being infinitely subtle? Was she just a catalyst? Did she wish to try to save me from what she almost had succumbed to herself? We were so close in these hours. I let the words fall into the conversation. "I feel very close to you."

"But, of course. We will always be close. I will want you to know my husband, my children, my lovers, my careers, my life. You'll see. This is only the beginning."

I wondered if she were accurate. People meet, their paths cross, they connect for a moment in time and then remain forever close even if far apart. They were always able to take up with each other even if years passed and they were no longer part of each other's lives.

"Let's drink to that. This is a true occasion."

We clinked glasses and then lingered over coffee. It was quite late by the time we returned to the apartment. I looked around for Don, frightened that he might be there. He was not. We walked up the stairs arm in arm, deliciously content.

The apartment seemed haunted. His presence was there. Though he was not there, we both felt that he was. We sat drinking for a while and then it seemed pointless to stay up.

"Are you tired?" I asked, concerned.

"Extremely."

"I've already made the bed. You'll stay in my room and I'll stay out here."

"You're welcome to join me, you know. Even if we just sleep side by side. It would be so comforting."

"I think not. Let's not complicate a beautiful evening."

She acquiesced, came over to me for a long and beautiful kiss, then slowly wended her way down the corridor to the bedroom. A moment later, she was back with me, wide-eyed, horrified.

"What's the matter?"

"He's there. In bed. Waiting for us."

Our worst scenario upon us.

"Shall I ask him to leave?"

"What shall we do?"

I offered to go in and speak with him. She acquiesced. I walked slowly down the corridor, in a state of panic.

He stared at me, satisfied with himself. What could I do?

"You promised me. You asked me to come to you. What happened?"

"I couldn't stay away. I tried. I just couldn't."

"Now what?" I almost pleaded.

"You decide. Put her out there. Or, both of you, come and join me."

"What do you have in mind?"

Don was determined. "I want to sleep with both of you. I've always wanted that. That will decide a lot of things."

"What could it possibly decide?"

"What our real relationship is. The meaning of it all."

46

"You think one mutual orgasm will solve it all?"

"Why not?"

"You're really very naïve, my boy. Sex is not the answer."

"Then it's the question. But it belongs in the equation, *n'est-ce pas*, as you French professors say?"

"You're going to louse up what was a beautiful evening."

"Well then, sleep with her yourself. I'll sleep on the couch."

"That's not what I mean. It's you I want. But she's a friend and she wants the best for both of us."

"Did you tell her about us?"

"Certainly not. That's our business. Our business alone."

"Well, let's enrich the experience."

"I'm not even sure we should. She just had an abortion."

"Well then, let's just spend a night in each other's arms."

"You're incapable of that. If you only could."

"I could."

"Well then, propose it to her."

"Okay. Tell her to come in."

"You go out to her. Make an effort. Be kind."

"I'm not dressed."

"Nudity is crudity, I understand."

He got up, put back his underwear and went out to her. Their voices were loud and somewhat acrimonious. I wondered if I should join them. Then I heard their steps coming down the corridor.

They were both in the door, Don with his arm around Anne.

"We've decided to join you," she said, with a husky voice.

"*Soyez le bienvenu.*" French was appropriate for such a moment.

I got up. Don lay down in the middle of the bed, obviously lucky Pierre. Anne lay down in the crook of his arm. After a moment, I joined them on the other side of Don. I was not really embarrassed by it all. It seemed inevitable once it started. We arranged ourselves in meaningful positions. There were so many possibilities. Would Anne and I be Don's lovers? Would Don and I share Anne? Would they be my lovers? We didn't have time to think about any of it. At one point, Anne was standing between us as we caressed her exquisite body. It was like a ballet and it was not so much sexual as erotic. It went on all night and exhausted us all three. Don was joyous, I was perplexed, Anne was silent, as if she knew the outcome of it all. Don cried with jubilation and proclaimed it the happiest moment of his life. At which time Anne's eyes met mine and we knew we would have difficulty disconnecting this incendiary threesome. I left the room and brought us champagne. We drank to our union and then fell asleep, she lying between us, Don with his head between her legs and I holding them both in a light embrace. Balanchine could not have done better, I thought.

Chapter Eight

In the morning, Anne and I found ourselves alone. While we slept, Don had absconded, just as secretly as he had come. Fortunately, we were both civilized. She prepared breakfast for us, made the bed, tidied up and proffered no perceptible comment. We were having coffee, it was shortly after nine in the morning and we were really rather comfortable with one another.

"I'm glad he's not here. I don't know what I would have done with him," she offered, pensive.

"That's probably why he left. He couldn't face the ultimate music."

She laughed heartily. "And we can, of course."

"We have to," I countered. "Someone has to."

"Well, at least we've been through the worst."

"The worst? It might have been the best," I countered again. "I wonder how we'll be able to live without each other."

"I for one will find it difficult."

"You're really years ahead of your chronological age. You're a most mature creature."

"So are you."

"Well, I should be, at my advanced age."

"Which is?"

"Thirty-three."

"That's not so very advanced." She leaned over to kiss me on the cheek. "More coffee?"

"Why not?"

We went on and on for a while. Then she took on a definite look. "I have decided to withdraw."

"Won't you stay the weekend?"

"I thought I would but I think it best not to. I couldn't live out another one of our orgies."

"Neither could I. And neither could Don."

"Oh yes, he certainly could. He's experimenting with his sexuality, with his identity. He keeps wondering whether he's a man or a woman, straight or gay, I'm sure. He's playing with fire. I'm certain he's having a major identity crisis. I know who I am and you, I presume, know who you are. But our little friend Don is playing a hell of a game."

"Are you sure we aren't?"

"Absolutely. If you brought me a young lady, a dowager or a monkey, I know I wouldn't want to go to bed with any of them. I have nothing against them, you understand, but I'm taken with men. I don't have any identity crises about that."

"Well bully for you."

"I better get out of here before I find out too much about you. I already know more than enough about dear Don. How did I ever get involved with all this?"

"Ditto."

"Well, I feel guilty running out on you both but I feel that you can handle him and I will be rooting for you all the way. I want you to visit me in a month or so and give me a progress report..."

"Anne dear, do you really want to keep knowing me, knowing what you do?"

"Of course. You're salvageable even if he isn't. In better circumstances, I might have made a serious play for you."

"I wish you had."

"Come now. I may be your junior by several years but I'm not a fool."

"We'll have long talks about it."

She brought out her suitcase. We drove to the station and kissed fondly, like the sudden old friends that we were.

Saturday afternoon. What would I do with it? Don was perhaps painting, as he said he would. I went home, changed into casual clothes and set out to find his cubby hole. The campus was huge and the basement of Weir Hall was filled with all sorts of work places. It was such a beautiful day that I couldn't imagine anyone hiding away from the sunlight. But there were quite a few weekend painters at work. I soon came on Don. He was absorbed in a rather flamboyant painting and he didn't hear me walk by. I came up behind him and tapped him on the shoulder. He half turned and went on working.

"Here I am."

"I knew you'd come."

"I had to take her to the station."

"You mean she didn't stay out the weekend."

"Did you expect her to?"

"I thought she might. It could have been a double header."

"You have quite an imagination."

"If you wanted her to stay so badly, why did you run off?"

"I couldn't face the two of you. I was ashamed."

"That was decent of you."

"How did you two face each other?"

"We were born civilized. We had several cups of excellent coffee and some good conversation."

"Well, you are more mature than I am. I had to have the consolation of art."

"Fortunate for you that you have it."

"You could have marked some papers."

"Don't be impertinent."

"She could have played a little *Carnaval*."

"You can be rather cold blooded."

I began leafing through some drawings Don had made. There was one that I particularly liked. It was the behind of a... man or a woman. The identity was unclear. "Is this a man or a woman?"

"Guess."

"I can't tell."

"That's the problem. What would you want it to be?"

"No more enigmas, please. Did you intend to draw a man or a woman?"

"I wasn't sure. That's my problem. Until recently, I thought I wanted a woman. I was sure of it. Then you came along and I wanted a man. I'm still not sure. Maybe what I want is a combination."

"With adjustable parts."

"Nothing so clinical. I don't want a hermaphrodite. I don't want a man who's really a woman or a woman who's really a man. I want someone who is someone. I want someone who makes me feel like a man."

"Do I make you feel like a man?"

"Sometimes. Not all the time."

"It's a matter of yin and yang. Sometimes men have more yang. Sometimes women do. Sometimes men have more yin. Sometimes women do. It's not really a question of sexuality. It's a matter of dominance."

"You must talk about that in class some time. Does Titus have more yin? Does Bérénice have more yang? Does Antiochus have more yin? Who dominates whom?"

"You read the play. I'm so pleased."

"I've read everything and I've thought about everything."

"Well then, my bright boy, who has the yang, Anne, yourself or me?"

"I've been wondering. Anne is all yin. You're yang and I'm floating between the two, with my wang."

"I wish you'd told me that long ago. I might have responded better."

"You responded well enough. You held me enthralled in your glance."

"How eloquent."

"You made me want you."

"You didn't want to do it."

"In a moment, we'll be writing a musical."

"Not a bad idea. We could go places."

"We have gone places. The question, can we live up to where we've been."

"Don, tell me, what is it that you want? If you know, I'll try to give it to you."

"For the moment, I think I want your love and your support. I want you to help me through this difficult period."

"How do you want me to help you?"

"I'm not sure. I just want to have the security of seeing you whenever I want and having your sweet body next to mine whenever I want it."

"And does it matter what I want?"

"You want me. I know that. You want me so much, it hurts. You'd do anything to keep me with you. Don't think I don't know."

"Then what's the problem?"

"The problem is time. I want you now. I want this life. But it's so different from what I hail from. My family would not survive if they knew about us."

"So would mine. We don't have to tell them."

"But there will come a time when we have to pleasure our families, when we have to become responsible members of society."

"I am a responsible member of society."

"You are but I'm not."

"You have a few years to go yet. At any rate, if you don't stay with me, you'll find someone else."

"So will you. We might both find women. It's easier with a woman, isn't it?"

"That depends on the woman."

"You could live with a woman like Anne. You could satisfy her family."

"Her family, perhaps, but not Anne."

"Oh yes, you could. She wanted you."

"Only before she knew we were together."

"We never told her."

"We never had to."

"She wanted you on a silver platter."

"Nonsense. As soon as she sensed that we were an item, she couldn't allow it."

"She just wanted to prove she was irresistible."

"There you're wrong. She's strongly sexed and needs a man. She might just have too much of an appetite. There's a bit of the nymphomaniac in her."

"All three of us have too much of an appetite."

"That remains to be seen. I don't think I do."

"I could awaken it in you. There must be a perfect mate for everyone in this world. Until you meet that person, you couldn't imagine what it would be like."

"You're amazingly astute for someone so unsure."

"It's only a matter of identity. I don't know for sure who I am. I thought I wanted Anne. I now think I want you. Who knows what might happen in a year's time."

"We all can change."

"I hope not."

We sparred on like this for a while. I sat there watching him absorbed in his painting, cleaning his brushes, working with the turpentine, mixing colors on a palette. I was more impressed by his drawings than his paintings. They didn't seem to represent him. His work was assertive, brash. His personality was so vulnerable.

"I'd like to pose for you."

"Whatever for?"

"To find out whether you'd paint a man or a woman."

"That's a nifty idea. It would probably depend on what we had done sexually the night before. That's what baffles me the most. Sometimes I want to penetrate you, to humiliate you. Sometimes I want you to master me. I'm never sure what I'm going to want you to be for me."

"That wasn't true with her."

"That's right. With her I had no choice. I was either the man or I was out. Odd man out."

He laughed, amused by his conjectures.

"But there are women who master their men. There are men who wish to be subservient to their women."

"We're not dealing here with perversity. We're not perverse. We're normal human beings."

"Normal," I blurted out. "How nice that normality can take on so many guises."

"So many geysers." We both laughed. So far out and not even drinking beers.

He started packing up his brushes. "I guess I've had it for today."

"Shall I get out of here and let you get some more work done?"

"No. I told you. I've had it for today. All this sexual psychology and role playing is making me nervous."

"What do you want to do?"

"Let's go back to your place and relax a while."

"You want to role play some more?"

"I don't want to think about it. I'll just let it happen. Maybe we'll try something entirely new."

"Maybe we'll just sit around and do nothing at all."

"Sounds wonderful."

We walked out together, arm in arm. I kept hoping nobody would see us. After all, he was my student. And then I realized I had made no real progress at all, inside of myself. I was afraid of what society would think. I was afraid for my reputation. I could never bring him home to my family or even my friends. And neither could he. Perhaps, one day, all this would change. Perhaps we could afford to be what we really were. Would that day ever come?

Chapter Nine

Rehearsals for *The Cherry Orchard* accelerated. There were only a few weeks between now and the first performance. The cast was on the qui vive. Carolyn and I bonded even more. She was playing silly Dunyasha, a role which Meryl Streep would one day make her own. I realized that Chekhov performances were dependent on their weakest and strongest links. It was all ensemble and one noticed what made it work and what prevented it from working. Our cast comprised of the choice dramatic elements on campus. I was playing Gayev, the errant brother, the cry-baby of the piece. He and his sister, Ranevskaya, were children who never grew up and who still lamented the loss of their mother and her angelic presence in the Cherry Orchard. One had to build each role. Chekhov did not tell you who each person truly was. The pauses between moments had to be filled with silent meaningful action.

Gayev had a marvelous moment in the first act. He made an extravagant speech to the venerable one hundred year old bookcase. It was one of the great monologues of the theater.

"Dear, honored bookcase."

Next year, I would use that to audition for study with the venerable actress guru, Uta Hagen. She accepted me as a student, "I think I can help you," she said, in typical dire Uta fashion. We both laughed heartily. Ralph Porter asked us all to study our roles carefully and to interpret them for one another and with one another. Each character had to be more than meaningful when the only décor was a maze of metal lines which served only to separate one actor from another. Gayev was nervous, childlike, a boaster, an inveterate talker, unable to stop himself, using all kinds of terms from billiards to mask his nervousness. He was in love with and ashamed of his profligate sister. He pardoned her everything. They both criticized one another mercilessly. She was the victim of a terrible romance in Paris. She loved him but he took all of her energy. She had continually to flee him. Then he would beg for her return. She would invariably go back. She would finish her days in Paris. Gayev would be with her, eventually. He had no life, except for his philosophical poses. He was a man of the Eighties. He was shamefully verbose and romantic. I sensed that he was probably gay. He had never had a romance with a woman and never dared to have one with a man. He hated Yasha though he was probably as attracted to him as Dunyasha was. Like Chekhov himself, he had never allowed himself to have an affair. He hid behind his love for beauty, but if push came to shove, and it never did in Chekhov's plays, he couldn't function with a woman. Chekhov might have had an affair with his publisher Suvorin, who lorded it over him but so many women were mad for him that enough of them convinced the world that he desired them as well. Some even said they had had affairs with them, but there was no proof. When Chekhov became too ill for it to matter, he married the actress who was closest to him (or was she?), Olga, who incarnated his leading roles and with his sister kept his name alive for a half-century after Chekhov's untimely demise in 1904.

"Gayev was gay," I said, when asked to say one major thing about the character we were incarnating. I was practically booed off the rehearsal stage, though everyone registered the possibility.

"Let us not be outrageous for the sake of being outrageous," our director cautioned us.

I didn't push my point. Everybody probably sensed that I was, though several women were as ready to protect my name as well as Johann's in the German department. Elspeth, my vis-à-vis, who played Ranevskaya and was one of the few who was at the proper age for that, gave me a most serious look and told me I was, "a brilliant boy".

I wished Don were one of the actors. He would have stood up for my version of it, or would he have? I would have to find the way to get him to see it or else read it to him in the near future. How many millions of unfulfilled people were just that way because they never found someone to love. They lived in a world of illusion and kept the truth from themselves so that they would keep it from their nearest and dearest. They devoted themselves to elderly parents, mothers, aunts, so as to avoid the search for the significant other, or as Don trippingly put it, the significant udder. We had so much fun punning. My father was an inveterate punster. I grew up with puns and coffee for breakfast and even such silly moments as being told I would be sent to Jail (Yale) if I were a good enough student. Don loved puns and did better at them even than I did.

I came back from rehearsal all tuckered out, as we said, found Don waiting for me on the stairs and told him what I had been through in the last hours.

"I'll check you out," he promised. "Just don't play obvious."

"Of course not," I insisted. In Europe, effeminate men are most masculine and heterosexual, especially in England. Homosexual men were often the most macho, especially in Germany and in the US. No stereotype ever worked. And how could one characterize the ambiguous deviant, the bisexual? Bisexuals were the most complicated. So many married and so many lived double lives. Especially the women. How many women preferred women and found it easier to have lives with men they liked. Under cover of marriage. We discussed all these things as if we really understood them. We went into the intricacies of the lives of the Duke and Duchess of Windsor. Every couple has a favored way of making love. If you find out what really pleasures someone, you can have them for life.

"I have a friend who is an astrologer and who maintains that he can tell you exactly what you desire and that most people don't even know unless they're fortunate enough to find it. And how few do."

"Life is an endless struggle to understand the simplest things," Don said, quietly. "I'm giving myself at least a year more to understand it all before I choose a lifestyle."

"But you might take many more years to understand. There are watershed years."

"I'm impatient. I give myself about one more year."

"I give myself a lifetime."

"That means you don't care to have a family."

"There are many ways of having a family. I certainly don't want what my parents had," I proclaimed.

"I do. What makes me hurt is that my parents had a good thing. I would never want to hurt them."

"But you have brothers and sisters. I don't."

"That's true. I have one of each but I don't want them to take the responsibility from me."

"You don't believe in destiny or serendipity."

"I'm trying not to. That's why I'm having difficulty with you. You're everything I never thought I'd have to face."

"Look," I said, sincerely, "it's not too late to break. We can still do it without too much pain."

"I said I'd give myself a year. Don't rush us."

"I may just give you a few months."

"I wish I could make you pregnant and we could have everything together."

"Men will one day adopt children."

"I don't want to adopt them. I want my own."

"Then find another Anne, impregnate her and ask to bring up the child with your male lover."

"That would have been a great idea. Who knows, that might be a possibility."

He came over to me, stood over me where I sat and held my head in his hands. "I wonder what we would have produced were it ever a possibility."

"That reminds me of George Bernard Shaw and Mrs. Patrick Campbell."

He was all ears.

"She was a beauty and he was an intellect. He resisted her offer. She had proposed a union which would lead to a child with his brains and her beauty. He countered: "But what if the child had your brains and my beauty?""

"I never heard that."

"Good. Every once in a while I can teach you something."

"That's your mission. You're the teach and I'm the student."

"But what we soon learn is that every teacher is instructed by his or her students. Teachers love teaching because they learn so much."

"To be an effective teacher, you must wish to learn."

"It's give and take all the way."

"What have you learned from me?"

"That teachers can be so cute." He tweaked my cheek.

"What have you learned from me?" Don gave me my chance to answer.

"That wisdom comes from the mouth of babes."

"Aren't you nice?"

"Try me."

"Try me," he insisted.

I rose into his waiting arms. We exchanged passionate kisses. I knew I was succumbing more and more to his charms and I felt part of a vortex of feelings. Yet I felt it would have an end, just as it had had a beginning. I did not yet allow myself to trust this maelstrom of desire. His effect on me was so powerful that I could come to orgasm just by being kissed. He insisted on this, exciting me as if I were a woman on the verge of orgasm. When I began to moan, he was fulfilled. He soon moaned in the same way, and neither of us needed to remove one piece of clothing. We were hopelessly hooked.

Chapter Ten

I decided to give a dinner party in honor of the opening of *The Cherry Orchard*. It would be a midnight supper after the end of the performance. Why would I complicate my life in this way? Actually, for several reasons, but mostly because the intensity of the relationship with Don was beginning to get to me. Sometimes I wished to wave a magic wand and end it, sometimes I thought I would scream from the housetops that I had a lover and would be happy forever.

I phoned Dana, who hadn't been in touch for some time. She seemed more morose than usual. I would get her out of her doldrums by asking her to help me with the party. Not even the possibility of that seemed to warm her cockles.

"I'm going to have a huge mess of shrimp. Would you help me clean them?"

"Of course, my darling. But I'm not sure I'll be here much longer, so make it soon."

"Next week. What's the matter?"

"Harry is getting on my nerves. He's investigating me and has turned up some of my activities."

"I always thought he had the mentality of the CIA."

"He does. But I've had it. One more bad moment and I intend to take a powder."

She arrived the morning of the dinner with a rather large suitcase.

"You're not moving in here, are you?" I asked, just in case.

"No, my dear. I'm going to clean your shrimp and tote your barge and make everything gorgeous and then I'm going to disappear. I ask only one thing of you. If the CIA interrogates you, say you know nothing."

"But you're invited to the party."

"I don't want parties. I just want to get out of here and lead a more normal life."

"But Dana, sweetheart, you can do that."

"Not with that horror lying next to me every night, wondering where I've been and threatening me with sanctions."

"He probably can't bear the fact that you make out with students. That's hard to take."

"Look who's talking."

I blushed.

"Don't worry. I'm more astute than most. And I'm not judgmental. If you're attractive, you're attractive at any age. Nice to meet them at any age."

"You're a wonderful woman."

"I should have married you if you were the marrying kind. That way you'd always have somebody around to clean your shrimp and your seafood."

"The only thing that ever frightened me were your tarantulas."

"They're my best friends. They don't take any nonsense from anybody."

"What do you intend to do with your life?"

"I'm going to find me a man, a real man, who can get it up any time of the day or night, and doesn't have any glorious notions about how wonderful he is. Then I'll be fine."

She worked swiftly and brilliantly, deveining and
shelling, shelling and deveining. I went out shopping and
left her mistress of the domain. When I returned, she was
gone and there was a sweet note from her. 'Mission
accomplished. I'm off to a better world. You never saw me.
A un de ces jours. Love, Dana. P.S. Break a leg.'

Chapter Eleven

The Cherry Orchard was a huge campus success. We were deluged with compliments. Don came back with the others and whispered in my ear: "You were great. I really thought you were in love with the bookcase. You played it for all it was worth."

I was genuinely happy. There is nothing like doing a good job and knowing it, then being congratulated by the person who means the most to you. I ran home first to get ready for the guests. Don said he would do the honors and greet them, leaving me with the food responsibilities. Carolyn came with me, as well. She was in fine fettle. I had only to be careful and not have her find out about Don. Because if she ever knew, the whole campus would find out. *Sotto voce.* What I didn't understand was that they probably all knew by now. On this campus, everybody knew everything about everything about everybody else. And if they didn't know anything, they would then make it up. So it was best to let them know something. This evening I wasn't afraid. I was surrounded by love and shrimp and I felt particularly invulnerable.

Barlow was leaning on the piano, his food plate resting securely on it. He was most imposing. I came over to him as I knew that he would pontificate something most meaningful. He was at his most affable.

"I didn't know you were such a fine actor. There seems to be no limit to your abilities."

"Coming from you, that's high praise. I'm particularly sensitive to Chekhov's work. I have a deep desire to retranslate all of his work."

"Bully for you. You should do it. We must all make our mark while we can."

"I have a feeling one day that I'll write plays and even an opera by the time I'm sixty. I'd also like to write the life of Caravaggio."

"That's splendid. Be sure to get to New York and keep on going. If you stay here, you'll be worn out."

"But I love it here. It gives me such a perspective. It's not easy to live in New York."

"It's not easy to live anywhere."

"I want to live where I have love."

"You're too young to be that sentimental. Love has its moment or moments. It never lasts."

"Isn't that a bit cynical?"

"Call it what you wish. You're still a young man. Ambition and love thwart each other."

"If it's a choice between ambition and love, then I'll choose the latter."

"You can have as much love as you want, if you're willing to pay the price."

"That I understand. It reminds me of one of Garbo's great moments. She finally finds love and confides to her lover: 'We'll pay for this.'" I imitated the deep throaty Garbo voice.

Barlow laughed. "You belong in that world. You believe in all those fabulous banalities."

"What do you believe in, Sir Barlow?"

"Read my next novel. If I ever finish it."

"I'm serious. Here I am with you at this moment and I'm speaking only to you. I need your wisdom."

"I believe in loyalty, family values, friendship, solid rock money and mothers."

"You're not an easy man to pin down."

"I've seen too much for too long. Have you any idea where Dana is? Harry can't find her."

I remained silent. "She's probably taken her tarantulas for a walk."

"I thought you might be in on her whereabouts since you're serving perfectly cleaned and deveined shrimp."

"She's not the only one who has that talent."

"Don't tell me you had time to act and to cook, as well."

"Cooking is a deep relaxation. My mother is the best cook in the world. I learned culinary discipline from her."

Don walked over to us with a huge plate of hors d'oeuvres.

Barlow helped himself to another group of tempting foods.

"May I get you a drink, sir?"

"Certainly. I'll have anything with gin."

"Name your poison."

"I'll leave it up to your judgment, young man. You seem to have an inordinate amount."

Don was working the room and doing well. Barlow looked him over as he circulated to the kitchen.

"Who's that? He's enchanting. And bright, as well."

"He's one of my excellent students. A talented musician and artist."

"I've seen him around. He hasn't taken any of my seminars, as yet. Send him to me some time."

"He's got a mind of his own."

"They're the ones I like. I don't enjoy the dependent idiots."

"I'll suggest it. But I think he's almost finished all his courses. He won't be here much longer."

"Rotten luck. If he needs an independent study of some kind, I'm available."

"I won't forget."

Carolyn came to us with her usual brio.

Barlow sent a few compliments her way, as well. "My dear, I never knew you were so talented. You really tickled my fancy. I'll congratulate Bill."

"Don't say a word to him. He thinks my theater activities are making me neglect our children."

"Isn't that their purpose? Theater people have no feeling for ordinary family life."

"That's pure nonsense," I objected.

Barlow insisted. "The theater is its own family."

"That's certainly true," came the authoritative voice of Elizabeth Schoen. "I enjoyed you both so much. The entire evening was one total enchantment. I don't know how you did it. No set, no atmosphere and yet Chekhov's spirit was entirely valid. People in New York or Vienna would scream at the tops of their lungs that Chekhov had been violated. But I for one understood immediately that you had caught the essence of the great Chekhov's heart."

Barlow gave her a challenging look. "You have the soul of a drama critic, my dear. I thought you only fathomed the ballet."

"They played it as if it were a verbal ballet. It was so graceful, so full of nuance, its own verbal music. Felicitations."

The enchantment of the evening continued. Compliments flew by and I kept thinking that this was one of the great moments of my life at the university. I would have to write about it one day. In perspective. But are we ever in perspective?

Later, after they had all gone their various ways and we were cleaning up the debris, munching on hors d'oeuvres, commenting on everyone's post-theater behavior, we sat and discussed it all.

"It wouldn't have been anything without you," I told Don.

"You're too kind. You survived all those barracuda. They really like you."

"They like me because they're not jealous of me. If I ever really succeeded in their worlds, they would tear me to bits."

"Well then, succeed after this period."

"That's what I intend to do. Or else what I would fear would happen."

"You have all the time in the world."

"We all think we do but I'm not sure we do."

"This is just practice time. Like Mariana Herzlich, you're still doing your time in Meedletown."

"In which world would you like to succeed?"

"I don't need success. I just want to lead a humdrum life, be a good citizen and make enough money to live it up here and there."

"Then why do you play music and paint?"

"Because it's not part of my future, irrevocably. I just want to know what it feels like. I have no illusions about triumphing in it."

"That's a cop out, isn't it? Why should I be more ambitious than you are?"

"Because you have ambition written all over you. You're just biding your time. Your day will surely come."

"Maybe I can breathe some ambition in you."

"Breed."

"You're so sensitive to language. One day you'll write something very important."

"One day I'll read something very important. That will be enough."

"Don't all these ambitious people make you nervous?"

"That's why I frequent them. I want to be nervous for a while. Not forever."

"Why did you ever start with Anne? Didn't you know she was ambitious?"

"She thinks she's ambitious, but she's only interested in impressing people. She'll always be on the periphery. She doesn't go deep enough."

"How can you know that?"

"You know things when you sleep with people."

"Things like that?"

"One night with someone and you can know everything."

"You never cease to amaze me."

"Stick with me, kid."

"That's what I want to do."

"Then behave."

"I am behaving."

"Good. Now let's listen to a little music and put ourselves in the mood for love."

"I'm always in the mood for love when I'm with you."

"I was afraid you wouldn't be. The play would go to your head and you would be unavailable."

"How could you think that?"

"I think a lot of things. I worry a lot."

"I worry a lot, too."

"Then let's put a moratorium on worry for now. Let's just enjoy the simple process of being."

"I think you'll end up being a teacher one day."

"No, I won't. I just want to make money and have a decent bourgeois life."

"Is that your ultimate ambition?"

"No. I want to be a solid citizen."

"Well, we have to have some of those, don't we?"

"I guess we do."

"You mean, all you want to do in the long run is pleasure your family and be a dyed in the wool bourgeois?"

"I'm not sure yet. But I don't think I have real talent for anything else."

"When I make it in those difficult worlds, I'll call you and ask you to join me."

"I'm not sure I have the courage for that. But I'll never forget you."

"I'll never forget you, either."

"Let's stop here, or I'm going to be maudlin."

We sat there in silence until the music stopped. Don got up to go to the john. Then he signaled me from the hall. I joined him. We walked down the corridor to the bedroom in silence, like two old friends. The phone rang.

"Must you take that?"

"I better."

I lifted the receiver. It was Anne's voice.

"Anne! How nice? Yes, tonight was the opening. How incredible of you to remember. Don and I just cleaned up the debris. I gave a dinner party afterward. And how are you?"

Don whispered: "Tell her I send my love."

"He sends his love."

A pause. "She sends hers as well."

"I'll give you a call one of these days when the great city beckons."

After I hung up, there was a momentary silence between us.

"You'll take up with her again one of these days."

"No, I won't. But if you ever leave me, she'll be my only witness."

"Good. I'm glad. I wouldn't want to abandon you completely."

"How thoughtful of you. Now shut up and make love to me, before I go to pieces."

We lay there in bed for a long time in total silence before one of us made a move. I was feeling dead tired. I wasn't sure I could make love at all. He obviously wasn't sure he could, either. We held hands in the dark and I sensed the tears that were falling from his eyes.

"What's the matter?"

"I'm making a mess of this. I don't know where this is all leading?"

"Just go with the flow."

"That sounds like one of my remarks."

"We both know each other's vocabulary so well by now that we could just reproduce it at will."

I wasn't sure which one of us fell asleep first. In the middle of the night we awoke and began to make love in a perfunctory manner. Would the day ever come when we no longer desired each other? Anything can happen. It was Anne's fault. She always put a damper on us. It was also Barlow's fault. Bits and pieces of conversation stick in your mind and ruin everything. The most important thing is to be together. Perfection is a rarity. I felt his lips on mine and the old desire came rushing and roaring back. Never be disillusioned. Desire is always there, just around the corner.

It was my turn to cry. Out of gratitude, out of hope, out of a realization that this was the nearest thing to paradise I might ever know. And I would have to struggle for that, despite all the fear, the anxiety, the negativity, the ultimate realization that every relationship was a deep struggle, a series of moments, a totality made possible by the will power of two different people always hoping to be one and always fearing to be inadequate to the task. Chekhov knew it was almost impossible. Yet Ranevskaya would return to Paris. And Varya would always alienate Lopahin. And the Gayevs of this world would be stuck with their ideals and their bookcases and their enthusiasms long after their lives had been definitively ruined. I held Don close. I would never let him go.

Chapter Twelve

Peter came for his desultory, occasional French lesson. I was in my office. I decided to greet him there rather than risk his arriving when Don was with me.

"I wrote your composition. I hope it makes sense."

"Good for you."

"We were studying Mérimée's *Carmen* and the difficulties it posed might help to teach Peter some more French.

"One thing you must understand, my friend, is that you have to begin to think in French rather than in English. We just don't think the same way the French do."

"You can say that again."

"For instance, here. You're talking about Don José. He fell in love with her."

"He sure fell for her."

"Yes, of course, but your French says: '*Il est tombé dans l'amour avec elle.*'"

Peter was insistent: "He fell in love with her."

I chuckled. "What you said was: He fell into love with her, as if he fell into a hole... do you understand?"

"Well, if you like, that's what happened."

"Yes and no. When the French say: he fell in love with her, they say: *Il est tombé amoureux d'elle.* It's not literal..."

"Well how should I know?" He was becoming more and more annoyed.

"Here's one that's even better. '*Il n'a jamais eu de l'amour par devant.*' I suppose you meant he never had loved before."

"That's right. He's a naïve kid."

"Yes, but what you actually said was that he had never had love in the front."

"Well, maybe his experience was up the ass, if you don't mind my meaning."

"That's possible, but what you meant was something else. You have to learn how the French say it. *Il n'a jamais fait l'amour avant.*"

"Those French. They don't care what they say as long as they pronounce it correctly."

"That's *My Fair Lady.*"

"I saw the musical."

"I think the French only think about sex."

"Maybe it's you who only think about sex, Peter."

"You have a point there." He rolled his eyes and gave a guffaw. "I don't think I'll ever learn French. My mind isn't dirty enough."

"It's dirty enough."

He gave me one of his total looks, fixing me in his gaze the way one looks at a butterfly that is about to be impaled.

"I told you. I'll do anything to pass. Name your price. I don't want to embarrass you. But I'll do anything. Don't make me write compositions. I'm not good at it."

"As I said to you Peter, if you make an honest attempt to do your work, you'll get through."

"What is an honest attempt?"

"What you're doing now. But you have to stop being defensive. You have to be willing to learn."

"Look. I am willing. But I know all there is to know about sex already. I don't need to learn it in French."

"You already know everything."

"You name it. I know it."

"Now you're shocking me."

"Listen. I'm a horny bastard. I've always been a horny bastard. Horny bastards get around."

"Around and about."

"If you like, I'll show you and you show me."

"Is that a proposition?"

"Not exactly. But if you show me how to pass French, I'll show you I appreciate it."

"We always get to the point, Peter, where it's better to stop talking."

"Whatever you like. But I have to get out of this damn college, pass French and go on to my next life."

"You've made that abundantly clear."

He took out a photograph and pushed it in front of my gaze.

"That's Susie. She's a great girl. She expects me to pass French. And I can't use dirty talk with her. She's too fine."

"I can see that. It's all right with me but not with her."

"You're one of the boys."

"One of the boys!"

"Don't take offense. You're practically our age. You're a regular fella. You're a good man. I can trust you."

"I'm glad to hear that."

"Well, we just have a few minutes. Teach me how to say something."

"What do you want to say?"

"Kiss me."

"*Embrasse-moi.*"

He tried the words out for size. "*Embrasse-moi.*"

"Fine, but you must be careful."

"Again?"

"*Embrasser* means kiss. But *baiser* as a verb means fuck. Penetrate."

"You mean, if you say: *baisez-moi*, you're being suggestive."

"That's right. As a noun, '*le baiser*' means the kiss."

I can't get over those French. No matter what they say, they suggest something else."

"Not always."

"Yeah, but there are limits. A kiss is not a fuck. A fuck is not a kiss."

"That depends."

"You know, I think you're either trying to annoy me or excite me."

"Why would I be trying to excite you, Peter?"

"I don't know. But when I'm with you, I feel like I'm about to make love."

"Why?"

"Don't ask me questions."

"Well, I should know what you're thinking, shouldn't I?"

"No, you shouldn't."

"I don't want to give you any false impressions, Peter."

"There's something about you, I don't know what it is, but you're as sexy as a girl. Do you know what I mean? I know you're a man and all that and you don't behave like a fag, but there's something so charming about you that you feel like there's nothing to do with you but screw you."

"The word screw also has double meanings, Peter. And I do not intend to get screwed by you, if you know what I mean."

"I'm not sure I know, but sometimes, late at night, when I whack off, if you pardon the expression, I find myself thinking about you."

"Peter, stop that."

"I don't mean anything disrespectful, you know. But you have a nice sweet little ass and a sexy voice. And then I get all embarrassed because I'm not gay, if you know what I mean, and yet there's something about you that makes me think we're going to end up in the hay."

Silence descended on the room. I was genuinely embarrassed. I sensed the purely animal quality he had. He had sensed something in me.

"May I ask you something, Peter?"

"Sure."

"Have you always felt this about me or did it just happen recently?"

"Come to think of it, I think it's recently."

It was then that I understood that I was secreting some extra something because of Don. I was communicating sensuality. Or perhaps it was because Peter was in love with his girl and that exacerbates one's sense of sexual attraction.

"Maybe it's because you're attracted to her."

"I don't think so. You don't remind me of her."

"It has nothing to do with that. We all exude certain things. Other people pick them up if they're receptive."

Peter just sat there. Then he got up and stared at me. I thought I was aware of a bulge between his legs. I had to get him out of there as quickly as possible. I couldn't handle this and I was sure he couldn't either.

"Peter, shall we continue these lessons or shall we forget about them?"

"We have to continue. Just hit my hand if I get fresh."

"I'll never hit your hand, Peter. Because you're not going to get fresh."

"If you keep looking at my crotch the way you do, I have no alternative."

"I'm not looking at your crotch, Peter."
"Then you must be cross-eyed."
"What do you want, Peter?"
"You know what I want."
"Well then, come and get it."

Peter walked toward me and then, suddenly, thinking better of it, he turned and fled. I was totally undone, frightened of myself, relieved that nothing had happened, knowing that it might very well have and probably would on another occasion. What would I do? I would be putting everything in jeopardy. If Don found out about it, he would reject me or perhaps just laugh. If Peter was afraid, he might tell someone. But he wouldn't. He depended on my benevolence. He was sure he had it. It was so different with him. It was pure unadulterated sexual stimulation. With Don it was love, it was tenderness, it was hostility, it was everything. With Peter it could never be anything but a kind of irritation. Sexuality was a form of irritation. Peter wanted to subjugate me, to show that he could be superior to me. And then I wondered whether Don didn't have many of the same feelings. With Don, words were everything. With Peter, words were only sexual signposts. I hoped he would not come towards me. Maybe he could simply masturbate himself thinking of dominating his French teacher.

Teaching was not an easy process. It was so close to forming an individual. It was an eternal seduction. That was why so many teachers and students had affairs. If they were at all sexually sensitive, the seduction was part of the ritual. That was why so many teachers and students bonded and sometimes made love and even married. Nothing is more intimate than a teaching situation. I felt like going anywhere to forget what I had just experienced. I went down to the local movie house, which was generally empty at this time of day. It was comfortably cool and one could forget just about anything there. I didn't even notice what was playing. I purchased a cool soda and sat down on the side in the back, not even seeing if anyone was there.

The picture was an old Tyrone Power flick. Tyrone Power was one of the sexiest. Here he was with Joan Fontaine and they were both so beautiful that I got myself all involved with them so that I would forget myself.

After a while, I began to see what was around me. Someone was sitting a few seats away and I thought I caught them staring at me, the way one does in dark movie houses, when one is cruising. Some moments later, he rose and came to sit next to me. He was managing a box of popcorn as well as a cold drink, which he perched on the edge of the seat. He turned and smiled at me and offered some popcorn. I was so taken aback that I accepted.

His right leg was moving slowly and imperceptibly towards my left leg. Before long, he had the calm audacity to press his leg against mine. He kept sneaking looks to see what my reaction was. I tried not to give any. Decidedly, I was secreting some sort of magic something that afternoon. Before I knew it, he had placed the soda and the popcorn on the floor. Now the suspense was enormous. The screen was filled with the romantic lovemaking of our hero and our heroine. His hungry hands placed themselves on my knee and he very slowly and surely moved them toward my crotch. He caressed it warmly and then zipped down my fly. He dropped on to his knees and slowly placed me into his hungry mouth. I was very frightened and did not dare to look directly at him or what he was doing. He didn't have to work too hard or too long. I came wildly and ejaculated into (was it Don? or Peter? or both?) the mouth that absorbed my nervousness. He sat up again and squeezed my arm, offered me some more popcorn and then got up and left. My heart kept beating fast for the longest time. When the film ended, I looked around and hoped I would see no one I knew. I was fortunate. I left and walked home in the crepuscular evening. When I reached upstairs I threw myself into bed and slept for a few hours. I made a solemn decision to go off to New York for the weekend and stay away from all of this.

Chapter Thirteen

I phoned Don to see whether he might like to spend the weekend in New York with me. It was a daring act since I had never proposed any voyage of any kind except vague allusions to the joy of sharing Paris. He always seemed theoretically receptive.

"Don, my dear, would you like to spend the weekend with me in New York?"

Silence. What might be termed a pause in a Chekhov play.

"What a nifty idea."

"Does that mean yes or no?"

"Neither yes nor no. What do you have in mind?"

"I haven't been there in weeks and weeks and I feel the need to get out of here. Why the French travel. *Pour changer les idées*, to get a new perspective."

"Do you need a new perspective?"

"I just feel like going."

"Then go."

"But I don't like leaving you."

"I would cramp your style."

"No you wouldn't."

"This way you could visit Anne. You could have a good talk."

"That's not why I'm going."

"I think I need to have a weekend by myself. It will do us both good. It really will."

"You won't be angry."

"Why would I be angry?"

"Because you're unpredictable and because I don't wish to displease you."

"You won't be displeasing me. You can tell me all about it. We'll have something to talk about."

"May I call you while I'm away?"

"Of course. I think I'll spend the weekend concentrating on my painting."

"That would be wonderful. I want to have one of your pieces and frame it."

"When I give it to you."

"If you give it to me."

"I promised you."

We gave each other more and more reassurances and off I went. Off and running. I decided not to take the car. I would just immerse myself in New York. I would perhaps not call anyone at all. Perhaps not even Anne. Especially not Anne.

It was early evening by the time I arrived. The crepuscular hour. The saddest hour of the day. That is why I would always try to teach between five and seven. Then I would be sure never to be alone at the hour of melancholy and sadness. At first it was exhilarating to walk all over New York without a destination. I said hello to the monuments. I waved hello to the lion in front of the library. I walked up to the park and walked along the lakes. I was invaded by nostalgia. The park reminded me of my childhood. I would go for walks with my mother and father. I was their prisoner. I saw so many young people and I could never meet anyone at all. I had no friends. I was an only child. We

only met older friends of theirs. I fantasized escaping. I
never had the courage. I never had a life. Now I finally had
it and I still did not do very well with escaping. I just fell
into routines. I walked over to the other side of the park. A
marvelous figure of a woman passed by. I knew who it was.
It was certainly Greta Garbo. They say she loved walking all
over New York. She passed by so quickly I wasn't sure.
Could she be as melancholy as me? That almost sounded
like a song.

Perhaps I would go see a Broadway show and then find
a place to spend the night. Perhaps the baths. Wonderfully
anonymous and so relaxing. I was out the other end of the
park and on Central Park West before I realized that this
must be near to where Anne lived. She always told me to
get in touch. I would call, just to say hello.

"Anne?"

"Darling. How are you? To what do I owe the honor?"

"I happened to come in town and I'm not far from your
place."

"Don't tell me. How extraordinary. I've been thinking of
you all day, wondering why and I thought of calling you.
Are you free?"

"As a bird."

"Well then, come right up. I'm expecting some people
later but we could have a long talk and drinks and you
could stay to dinner. I'd love to cook something for you. I
always promised. Incidentally, are you with Don?"

"No. He didn't wish to accompany me."

"How are the two of you doing? Don't tell me. We'll
catch up."

"Can I bring you something?"

"Just yourself. When can I expect you?"

"Give me a half an hour. To reconnoiter."

I walked right up to the house and decided I couldn't come empty handed. I walked around to a more busy thoroughfare on Columbus Avenue and found a liquor shop. I would bring her my favorite wine, a Volnay. And perhaps, a Vouvray, sparkling, lovely light Vouvray. I knew she liked that. It was amazing how much we had exchanged in our few conversations.

The lobby of her house was like that of an old mansion. I was entering a new world, one that I had never lived in Queens or the Bronx. It was life in the big city as so few New Yorkers know of it. The elevator operator had his regalia on. I was dropped on the eighth floor and wondered which apartment it was. He pointed to the one at the left. There were only two. How huge these apartments must be.

I waited a moment before ringing. I had to get myself together. I wondered if I would pass muster. The maid answered. She was a Filipino and loved to giggle. Miss Anne would be out in a moment. Would I care to have a seat in the salon? I walked straight ahead of me, down a corridor filled with books and records, a world of culture. Ahead of me was the salon with its grand piano. The walls were virtually empty. There was one painting and I wasn't immediately able to decide what it depicted. It was like an uncharted land in an obscure wood. I finally realized it was the legs of a woman and the hairy forest which existed between her legs.

It was the most suggestive painting I had ever seen. How different from the portrait of a gipsy woman my mother had exhibited in her living room, and which still was my referent for women. She had a sweet bohemian face and deep, dark, meaningful eyes. She was what the late 1890s would have called suggestive, just about as suggestive as a portrait of a white angora cat. The cat was my constant companion throughout childhood. But I never had a real cat. My mother would never allow a real pet in the house. When I rescued a cat from the street, I hid it under her bed. She found it and banished it. Six months later I became wildly allergic to cats. It took years to understand I was really allergic to my mother. It took at least two decades to realize that. Anne's suggestive painting was probably an index to her bohemian life.

I sat on her spotless white couch and felt as if I might be soiling it with the presence of my body. The art deco lamps and the magnificent fireplace were all signposts of another era. The apartment was spotless and elegant, probably the most elegant room I had ever seen. There was a silence in this room which belied the laughter of the Filipino girls emanating from the kitchen. At last, I heard the sound of footsteps. There she was, tall, thin, elegant, dressed in silk, all in white like the furniture.

"It's you. I couldn't believe it. What joy!"

"Here you are in your habitat. I'm so glad to be with you."

"I can't really believe you're here. You must promise me that we'll always be part of each other's lives."

"I promise."

"Are you hungry? What would you like to drink?"

I gave her my votive offerings. Volnay and Vouvray.

"You shouldn't have. Which would you like?"

"No. That's for you. I'll have a vodka on the rocks."

"Splendid. And I have some caviar my father brought back. How do you like your caviar?"

"Any way at all."

The girls brought out a silver tray with ice cold vodka from the fridge. The caviar was served on black bread, very thinly sliced. There were little bowls of slivered onions and hard boiled eggs. I wasn't sure I had ever had such a wonderful moment. Anne insisted on serving me.

"I miss you and Don, you know. I wish he liked me better. I would have hung around with you both but I couldn't. I tried."

"He was jealous of you."

"He'd be jealous of anyone. He wants total control."

"I'm not sure I understand him. He's taken hold of my life but I don't know for how long."

"He's an enchanting boy. He makes love like an angel but there's a devil in him, too, and he's never sure which will take over."

"I'm giving it this year. And so is he. We'll see if it's possible to make a go of it."

"I hope for your sake. It will be difficult when it's over."

"How do you know?"

"I sense these things. That's why I got rid of his child. I could have had it. I felt so guilty placing myself in the hands of my parents. I could have gone off to Europe or even to the west coast, had the baby and then figure out what to do. I could have tried to make a life with him. But I knew he didn't want me. As soon as he met you, he wanted to hide behind you."

"But that may be what he's doing. Hiding."

"He's not ready to face life after college."

"I don't think I am, either."

"You'll be all right. You'll come back to New York and start a real life. With a real person."

"How do you know?"

"I've lived a lot. I've seen a lot. Sometimes I feel a hundred years old."

"You really are enchanting. The mystery woman. When are you going to settle down with someone?"

"I have several options. I have a professor of my own who wishes to join with me in holy matrimony."

"Will you do it?"

"He's too possessive. He wishes to rule with an iron fist."

"Is it possible to find someone who isn't jealous?"

"I'll spend the rest of my life locating that. Because that's what I want. A man of the world. A man who has a genuine life of his own which would include me but not minimize me."

"Come to think of it, we both want the same thing."

"We're very much alike, my dear. I knew that immediately. I wish you were my brother. The brother I never had."

"The sister I never had."

"I thought you wanted more."

"I have nothing against incest."

"Almost all relationships are incestuous."

"That would be worthy of a long talk. We're about to be invaded, dear. There is a famous writer who's after me and he's going to drop by. We'll have dinner, the three of us, or more of us, if he comes with a friend. Then he and I will surely hit the hay and you can spend the night, as well. There's plenty of room."

"Are you sure? I can always go off."

"I wouldn't hear of it. If he hadn't said he was coming, I would have seen only you. But every once in a while one gets a chance to enlarge one's acquaintance meaningfully. This man doesn't like to be rejected and he's only in town for a few days. I met him at a cocktail party recently. He's a Czech expatriate and very important in his own literary world."

"I wouldn't cramp your style."

"You won't be doing that. In fact, it will be perfect. He will see that I'm not easy to reach, that I have my own entourage. It was a stroke of genius to have you here. You might enjoy meeting him, though we shall have to speak Russian together, or French, or whatnot. His English is rudimentary."

"I speak Hungarian."

"Then we're triple threat."

Her friend arrived as predicted. He was dark and unruly, straight as an arrow and deeply annoying. Anne seemed to enjoy him greatly. I could feel him plotting ways to get rid of me. I went to the john to give them time to plan their evening. When I returned we were brought to the table and served a delicious home meal. Leg of lamb, creamed potatoes, excellent string beans. A perfect salad with vinaigrette. The Volnay was served and I was complimented. We all spoke French. The time flew by and we found we were discussing French writers. Never had I heard Gide and Sartre commented on with such panache. I had never read a line of the playwright's work; it didn't seem to matter. Chekhov was a perfectly valid subject, Gorky as well and I found that I could function at one of these gatherings with no difficulty. After a wonderful crème caramel, we repaired to the salon and Anne sat down to play. A little Chopin, some Liszt, even Schubert. Then a bravura performance of Schumann's *Carnaval*. I would have her up to the college to play this. I reiterated it. We both told her she was an artiste manquée. Why hadn't she gone on to the concert stage? She didn't answer but then sat down with him and I once again realized that it was time for me to go to the john.

When I returned, they were in each other's arms. He had taken off his jacket and they were making serious inroads on their intimacy. I could now just slip off into the night. I was afraid we would become a threesome à la Don and I couldn't face that. Though I would certainly like to see her making love. I had a genuine desire to see her naked. I probably was a voyeur at heart. Before I had an opportunity to decide what to do, he lifted Anne up in his arms and deposited her on the rug in front of the painting. They began making love seriously. They had forgotten I was there. I got up and went into her private bedroom. Why hadn't they just gone to bed? The Filipino girls had let themselves quietly out and the place was as silent as a trysting place.

I stood at the window of her bedroom looking out at the park. The lights made the park infinitely beautiful. This was the intimacy of New York. If only I were not alone. Suddenly I thought of Don. I would try to call him. He would be impressed by a phone call. If I could find him. Who knows what he was doing?

I called his dorm and there was no answer. Which didn't mean anything. I should have known it would be impossible to reach him. He was perhaps out somewhere or playing some music. Was he thinking of me? Did I really play a part in his life? Something made me call my own place, as if that would bring me some consolation.

The phone rang three times and then the receiver was lifted. I said hello.

"Oh, it's you."

"Don! What are you doing there?"

"I hope you don't mind. I got lonely for you and I came up the stairs, as if you were there. I let myself in. I was thinking about you, conjuring you up and now you called. I feel positively powerful. How's New York?"

"Nothing without you. I wish you'd come with me. I'm so lonely for you."

"I thought you needed some time by yourself. I was hoping you'd call."

"What shall we do? Shall I come back? I could be there by morning."

"Suit yourself. We don't seem to be able to get on without each other. I do love you, you know."

"Did you paint?"

"I did, a little. But I found it hard when you weren't going to be showing up."

"I'll be there tomorrow evening."

"Can we have dinner together."

"Anything you say."

"Where are you spending the night? Alone, I hope."

"I'm at Anne's."

"I thought so. If she touches you, I'll scratch her eyes out."

"Don't worry about her. She's making love on the living room floor with a famous expatriate Czech playwright. I'm in another room. It's really very nice here."

"I should think so. Poor little rich girls live in nice places."

"They certainly do. You know, Don, she's really a lovely girl. And she's very hospitable."

"And so bohemian."

"She's not interested in me. She only wants my friendship."

"That's what they all say."

"Scout's honor. She just feels comfortable with me, as if we were brother and sister."

"I believe you. Don't insist too much. Just come back to me soon."

"I will, my love. I will."

"Goodnight. Happy dreams. I'll spend the night cuddling your favorite pillow."

"And I'll be thinking of you."

We tore away from one another and I would have to offer Anne some money for the long distance call. She would laugh. I decided not to look in on them again. I stared out the window for a long time. How I loved the tranquillity of a New York night, so full of sensuality and deep warmth. I would have to find the way to bring Don into this and show him it was not a threat. I fell asleep imagining what it would be like to be making love in this room or even on Anne's sensual rug. What fun! Life could be so beautiful, if we didn't muck it up. I felt so much at home in this oasis of freedom. My life was shaping up and I would try to share it meaningfully with Don. I would certainly share it wildly and meaningfully with Anne. I would have to suppress the loneliness and the Peters and the provocations. I would find the way. There was plenty of time. I fell asleep fully dressed, in case they would find their way into the bedroom. I dreamed that Don and I were in a mythical city wandering about, holding hands. We came on Anne and a man making love in the bushes. They smiled and waved and I was suffused with happiness.

Chapter Fourteen

I came off the train more than nervous. Anne had tried to dissuade me from leaving. Her latest vis-à-vis had left early in the morning. She had a bit of a hangover and would have loved to spend the weekend with me. I explained to her that I had found Don chez moi and that he had practically insisted that I return.

"I can see that claiming you is a full-time job. But you'll be back and next time I won't let you go so easily."

"I'm very grateful to you. You saved me last evening."

"And so did you... save me. I have a penchant for trying new men out and I ought to discipline myself a little better. Every man is a challenge."

"I understand. That will end some day when you can choose one over another."

"I'll still want them all," she said, provocatively.

"I'll write the story of your life. When you reach one hundred, we'll do it up proud."

"I have a feeling I'll do that rather soon. I don't stay with any of them."

We parted like the cohorts we were. She drove me to the station and held me hostage for a lovely lunch at the Oyster Bar in the Plaza. Everything she enjoyed, I enjoyed. I knew I'd be back. She left me with one cautionary word: "Don't let him hurt you."

I promised not to.

I spent the train ride thinking how I would approach the next days. I would be totally lovely to Don. I would avoid Peter if he didn't avoid me. I would write some letters, plan some classes, get ready for the end of the semester as best I could.

Nothing conclusive went through my head. Part of me realized I should have stayed in New York and continued my evasion of Middletown. It was very difficult to belong to two worlds. It was difficult to choose which world. I always had been and wanted to continue to be a New Yorker. That was what Barlow had tried to tell me, to escape before it was too late. I could never become a fixture at this noble college. It was a divine place to be. It would always be memorable but it was one scene in a lifetime. And Mariana Herzlich had certainly been right. However, the nearer I came to reunion with Don, the nearer I was to a situation I had to solve, that we had to solve together.

He was waiting outside the station in his car. I slid in beside him and off we went to the apartment. As soon as we had crossed the threshold, he took me in his arms and we held each other so close that neither of us could breathe. He had cleaned up and he sat me down on the couch, handed me a beer and put the Brando record on. Propped up on the chair facing the couch was the drawing of the half-man, half-woman, framed, obviously for me.

"It's beautiful. May I keep it?"

"Of course. I inscribed it."

It said, cryptically. 'In memoriam. Love, Don.'

"I'll always keep it. I'm so very touched."

"I'll give you others. I'll give them to you all if you want them."

"I'm glad you said love."

"I meant it."

"That's why this is such an important experience. Because it's love."

"Why do you say that?"

"Because with most young people, it's just sex."

"Sex without love is nothing."

"That depends on how you feel about sex. Some people dote on it. As La Rochefoucauld put it, there are those who might never fall in love if they hadn't heard about it. But then he confused the two. There are those who never make love but once they've had it, they want more. The appetite comes with the eating."

"Yes, professor."

"And there's the novel you must read, by Benjamin Constant. *Adolphe*. Adolphe was a young man who didn't feel any love. But his friends all fell in love and so he felt he had to, as well. And he chose an older woman named Ellénore. She loved him too much. He couldn't reciprocate. He ended up by hurting her so badly that she died of it. Not everyone has a talent for love."

"Lend me the book."

"I'll give you a copy. You must study it."

"I didn't know we would be having a class today."

"Forgive me. I was born didactic."

"I hope you gave Anne a few lessons, as well."

"She's the one who gives the lessons. But I'm afraid her talent is for sex, not love."

"You're as good a student as you are a teacher."

"But she has a lot to offer. She has a true talent for friendship."

"As you do."

"And what about you?"

"I have a talent for feeling. For experimentation."

"For love."

"Let's not exaggerate."

"You have so many talents, you don't know what to do with them."

"You are generosity itself."

"I know what I'm talking about, Don."

"If we go on like this, we'll be making testimonials, both of us."

"I just want to enjoy your company, to bask in it."

"As do I."

He lay his head on my shoulder and we sat there listening to the complete record. I placed his hand in mine and we were at peace.

We walked down the corridor and decided to take a shower before we merged. I felt fresh and refreshed, as I hoped he did. We lay in each other's arms and watched the sun go down. Then we made love for a time and even fell asleep for a moment or two.

"Shall we spend the entire evening like this," he inquired, "or shall we go out to dinner? I kept thinking I would take you to a fine dinner."

"I'd like to do what we did the first time we met. Go have a pizza and then drive back. Or we could drive out to a lookout and neck in the car like any other young couple."

"What if the police found us?"

"We could keep a watch out."

"Well, it's pizza time. I'm touched you remembered."

"I've never forgotten one moment of this adventure."

"Neither have I."

We drove out to the pizza place. It was not quite as full as it was late at night. We watched the pizza maker twirling his pizzas and he seemed to recognize us. He started showing off to exaggerate his virtuosity. He winked at us.

Don looked at me looking at him and wondered, I thought, whether he could be a threesome with us. I hoped not.

Right in the middle of our repast, as we were guzzling our beers, Harry walked in with Johann and his young friend. They were delighted to notice we were there. I was nervous for at least two reasons. I wondered how much Harry knew about my relationship with Dana. And I wondered how much Johann understood about my relationship with Don. I tried not to speak to them. But they tried to catch my eye.

Johann came over to our table and said hello.

"There you are. Would you like to join us?"

Don gave me a cautionary look.

"Many thanks, but I just can't. We're having a planning meeting." (As if we were planning some activity on campus.)

"How's Harry?" I added, on a human note.

"He's hurting. He wondered whether you had heard from Dana."

"Not me. I wish I had."

"Everybody thought you might have. She liked you so much."

"What happened to her?"

"She left Harry."

"Whatever for?"

Johann became confidential: "They weren't made for one another. It's like the Iris Murdoch novels. The men stick together and the straight couples unravel."

I could have killed Johann. I didn't want Don to think I had been indiscreet. Don made a move to go. "Perhaps I'm de trop."

I protested. "Certainly not. I'll say a word to my friends before we go." And then to Johann. "Tell Harry I'm devastated but I can't help him. See you in a while."

I waited until Johann was out of earshot and reporting back to his table.

"Perhaps we should have gone elsewhere."

"I hope they're not gossiping about us."

"Are you crazy? Johann and his friend are a known couple on campus. And Harry, who's a closet queen, just got left by Dana, as I told you."

"Well, you can go right over to them if you feel it's necessary."

"We'll stop by their table on the way out. That will do it."

"You're sure?"

"I have no interest in joining them. You can be assured of that."

"I guess we should get out of here soon."

"I hope they haven't ruined your evening."

"Our evening."

The pizza maker came over to our table and introduced himself as Antonio. We complimented him on his talent. He basked in the compliments.

"I've seen you guys before. You're good customers."

"We've only been here once before."

"Then you must have made an impression on me."

"Your pizzas certainly made an impression on us."

"Only my pizzas?" We both were embarrassed as hell.

"I get off around eight o'clock tonight," he proffered. "What are the two of you up to?"

Don rushed to answer. "We've got a date." And then he winked.

"That will confuse Antonio. Unless you want to invite him back to the apartment. We seem to be doing it to everybody this evening."

"I think we better get out of here," I countered, "Before things get really rough."

We asked for the bill and paid it quickly. We stopped for a moment to commiserate with Harry and to introduce Don to them all.

By the time we got to his car, I felt as if we had escaped a difficult situation.

We both laughed and laughed all the way home. There was a small part of both of us that would have wished to find out what would have happened, had we been accompanied by Antonio. But then Harry and Johann and company would have certainly seen us leaving together and there would possibly have been a major scandal in some element of the campus. This was certainly something that would not have happened in New York. We never stopped laughing all evening long and we ended up going to bed without making love. The whole thing had been so exhausting. And the pizzas lay heavily on our tummies.

"'Life is too short to spend two nights in Meedletown' echoes in my ears." Don said the words, distorting them. "Life is too short to eat two pizzas in Meedletown."

Chapter Fifteen

Don lay in bed cross-legged, his legs entwined in mine. Our faces were right up against each other, as if we were Siamese twins facing one another. We were not practicing some ancient rite from the Kama Sutra. We were facing one another as intimately as two people can. We allowed each other to kiss our foreheads, our eyelids, our mouths, our chins, our necks. We rubbed our hands all over each other's bodies, slowly and knowingly, exciting each morsel of each of our bodies. Our penises strained with desire but did not come to climax. They too touched in a fraternal intimacy. We locked knees and shoulders, tummies and teats. We stared into each other's eyes with an infinitely penetrating gaze. Our seriousness was so total that we were transported to another world. Which of us would come to climax first, barely moving, barely breathing, barely aware that we were merging our bodies as well as our souls. He began to shake and then I joined him, our collective sperm pouring forth out of our receptive bodies. Never had we been so intimate before. We were amazed by our total union. Our hearts beat in unison. Our souls joined. Our bodies and lips trembled. Could we go any further than this, two individuals joined at the hip? We allowed our tears to flow in an ecstasy that would soon elude us unless we were indeed fortunate. Gurgling noises came from our throats and we exhaled as if in an orgasm that would never end. We separated and each of us towards a different wall. Our buttocks touched discreetly and we lay there tasting the joy of separateness after the ecstasy of unison. We were so moved that we had no need of conversation. When we rose, we drank a silent cup of coffee. He waved to me cavalierly as he ran down the stairs. I tried valiantly to get ready for my day, knowing that I would not be able to relate to anything but the ecstasy of the night. We would have to return to normalcy and forget what rarely ever happened, the mingling of two bodies and souls in an *entente* which was more than *cordiale*.

I dressed in a silent ritual, gathered some books and made ready to go by organizing everything within my favorite briefcase. I knew that I had arrived at a new plateau of my existence, something very few people had ever reached. I had reached a form or fulfillment and then total nirvana. I was beyond fear. I was ready for a new existence. Day one of the new existence. Post-nirvana.

As I set forth, I got halfway down the stairs when smiling judas Peter appeared on the scene. He barred my way, smilingly.

"I'm sorry, I'm afraid I didn't behave very well last time. I came to apologize."

"No need," I said. "But please don't just show up; make an appointment."

"I can never find you. I was afraid you were no longer on campus."

"How could you think that?"

"I was afraid I disgusted you and that you had quit."

"I hardly think so."

"Then forgive me. I didn't mean any harm. Please give me another lesson. I'm willing to work. Tell me that there's hope for me."

"There's hope for you."

"Then can I have a lesson?"

"What do you want to learn?"

"I want to learn all about you."

"Why?"

"Because I never met anybody like you before. You turn me on."

"I thought you were turned on by a certain young lady."

"Yes, of course. But she's my future."

"That should be enough for you."

"You're my present."

"Peter, you're waxing eloquent."

"I have my moments."

"Peter, I don't have time now."

"Yes, you do. Trust me. Spend a moment with me. Give me a half hour. I'll do my best."

"I know you will. That's what worries me."

"*Baisez-moi.*"

"Stop kidding around."

"I mean it. *Baisez-moi.*"

"*Baise-moi.* It's more intimate."

He took my briefcase and ran up the stairs with it. I ran up after him. "Peter, now stop this. You're riling me."

He laughed, enjoying his moment. He sat down on the couch and dared me to come for it.

I sat down opposite him and drank down some more coffee. Most of me did not believe this was happening. He rose to get some coffee in the decanter and we drank our coffee in silence.

"*Baise-moi.*"

"Peter, stop being ridiculous please. You don't know what you are suggesting."

"Yes, I do."

"This is the last time I'm going to tell you to stop the nonsense."

"You're making my balls hurt."

"How poetic."

"You're hurting me. I'm not used to having to fight for what I want."

"I'm very tired, Peter. I've had it. You're ruining my day."

"Just give in and you'll see, all will be well."

"I give you five minutes to get out of here, or I'll do something drastic."

"I know how you feel. But I'll make you so happy, you won't feel that way any more."

"I'm going to count to ten."

"One–two–three—"

I felt the thoroughness of my foolishness. I knew he had won the battle. All I would have to do was to submit. That was all. We were past the point of fear. "Lock the door, Peter."

He obeyed and then went into the bathroom in the corridor.

I thought of running and disappearing somewhere.

Foolishness. He came out of the bathroom in the altogether. He was a big boy. He had none of the discretion of Don's body. His was the body of a football player, huge protruding buttocks, power knees, gorgeous huge cock, ample balls, sensuous mouth. He came up to me and fell on his knees.

I didn't budge, totally mesmerized. He picked me up and carried me into the bedroom, practically throwing me on to the bed. He quietly removed all of my clothes, piece by piece and kissed my neck and shoulders with princely abandon. He lifted my legs into the air and placed them on his shoulders. His beautiful member began to press quietly and surely into my welcoming behind. He went slowly and safely, surely penetrating me, using his spit to lubricate the entrance. I nearly fainted with pleasure as he sought his own, with more and more insistence.

After we had finished, I thought I should bring a little levity into the moment. It couldn't be taken seriously. "Quite a technique."

"I told you. I mean it. *Baise-moi. Baise-moi*, baby."

"Well, now you're ready for graduation. And better things."

"There will be none of that until I satisfy you that I know French."

"I'm satisfied."

"No, you're not. I am but you're not."

"There are all kinds of satisfaction in this world. It takes a while for two to tango."

"Yes, well, this was lesson number one in the sensual gambit. You give me one. I'll give you one."

"This one is sufficient. Sufficient unto the day."

"*Voulez-vous coucher avec moi?*" He said that with pride.

"*Oui, monsieur.*"

He had his clothes on in record time and was on his merry way. I was grateful for only one thing, that Don had not returned. I was more and more confused, desiring two men, wanting to get away from them both, wishing to merge with them both, wondering whether I would ever be able to sort this all out. There was too much simultaneity, too many juxtapositions. Life was one long juxtaposition. We would always be going from one experience to the next, always trying to understand the shape of the day, the meaning of the moment, wondering what the purpose and the meaning of sexuality was. Even Anne would be baffled by such experiences. Even she might never have had them. And yet she certainly did. A woman's wisdom could handle it all better. A woman was more complete. A man who was violated, penetrated, became a surrogate woman, did he not? Or did it all mean something else? We were all searching for our ideal mate. We had lost that many centuries, eons ago. Our Platonic other halves were waiting for us somewhere. Would we locate them in this lifetime? Could we somehow find them and live a happy, fulfilled existence?

Chapter Sixteen

Beatrice had a whole bunch of us up to tea. I always enjoyed spending time with the ladies at the university. They were a superb lot and each of them had something marvelous to contribute. I sorely missed Dana, who no one else missed. But there were quite a few others who had styles of their own.

Beatrice was a sophisticated low-key lady from the Netherlands. She smiled wanly and never pushed herself in any way. One could sense that she had led a life of service. She loved her husband, an intellectual, with genuine compassion for a man who never thought of anyone but himself. She produced a handsome son who would do them both proud. Everyone on campus loved her. She spent most of her time with Paul Barlow since she enjoyed his wry sense of humor.

She was also occasionally seen with handsome, eclectic Andrew, a Canadian economist who was always looking for a ten. He was incapable of fidelity which wasn't a terrible thing, but he always had to confess to each and every one of his banal infidelities and talk about them not only to his wife but to all of his friends. His wife accepted all of this with rare compassion for the stupidity of her husband. It was as if she couldn't face leaving him. Finally, when he and his daughter went off alone on a camping trip, there was a dreadful accident. The daughter fell to her death and

Andrew shouted *mea culpa* to all of his friends and his wife. The infidelities had not fazed her but the confession that he had been responsible for his daughter's death left her suddenly free. She left him and divorced him promptly. Beatrice was Andrew's confidant during this time. Undoubtedly she slept with him to make him feel as if nothing was his fault. The more he proclaimed his guilt, the less he seemed to believe in it. How many wives have had to fend for their husbands and forgive their stupidities. There were some handsome men who never were without consolation. Andrew could find a bed partner any day of the week. I was very fond of him, as well, had traveled to Europe with him one summer and had a short flirtation. Fortunately, I didn't take him seriously. Sometimes he would have slept with anything, just to be able to distance himself from his multifarious guilts. I often wondered how many wives and mistresses and lovers and children he would accumulate. Oh, Andrew, how fortunate you are, I often thought. You'll never be without.

Beatrice had invited a host of the ladies to her tea. She also peppered the moment with three of her most attractive men, none of whom preferred women: Paul, Johann and Edward Wallace. The straight ones would probably have disliked the whole occasion. It smelled of a private rally. Carolyn was there, of course. She was always one of the boys, rarely one of the girls, but Beatrice liked her because she was outspoken and scrupulously truthful. Elizabeth Schoen was invited because she lent class to an occasion. Nobody fooled her, either. There was also Mary Thornton, a delightful Australian woman who not only had the most delicious Australian intonation but also a cheery nature and a forgiving heart. She was related to one of Australia's prime ministers and she had married one of the gentlest and brightest of psychology professors. She was a doting mother and she placed her family first in all things. I always thought she was one of the only faithful people on campus. She probably never had a single unfaithful thought in her life.

I often wondered whether infidelity was inherited or was simply the product of insecurity as a child. There was nothing wrong with infidelity. One could be faithful even if one were unfaithful. The most important thing was to protect one's mate. If infidelity occurred, it was not to be talked about. If it happened, it could be denied. It could be denied even if it were eminently obvious. The most important thing was to protect the feelings of one's husband or wife. I was convinced that nothing ended a relationship other than hatred or indifference. Even hatred could keep two people together as they would never lose interest in hurting one another.

In New York, one could not imagine all this as clearly as it happened at the university. The small townness of it all made things clearer and sharper. I loved analyzing the dramatis personae, wondering what they were really like and why they were what they were. There we were: Beatrice (unfaithful to husband, deeply faithful to friends and lovers), Carolyn, (unfaithful in spirit but not in body), Mary (totally faithful in all things), Elizabeth (faithful now in older age but perhaps not earlier: who could ever tell?). And there were others, Ann (wife of famous alcoholic writer Carstairs), who was perhaps too worried about her husband's life and career to react to his wild drinking. He probably never had time to be unfaithful and therefore she never needed to be, either. And Elspeth, who played Ranevskaya to my Gayev. She was an elderly woman who adored her husband and understood everything there was to the notion of infidelity in a literary manner, but had probably never been unfaithful, herself. Dana would have been best of all. She would sleep with anything that moved and she preferred them young and feisty. Students were always better than faculty. Finally, add beautiful June, a woman who lived for her husband and their three children. Her husband was only human and strayed once or twice in their marriage. She forgave him even though the revelation of it all just broke her husband's spirit.

There were only three men, and we could analyze them in terms of infidelity, just as well. Johann was handsome and faithful to his young lover, a student, and flirted with every well-placed and well-heeled woman on campus. He fooled many of them. Paul was everyone's guru. He had had only one woman in his life, his rich mother and he never really had a talent for seducing the young men he desired but was deeply respected by everyone on campus because of his iconoclastic nature. Add one more besides myself, Edward Wallace, the Italian professor, an exquisitely intelligent gentleman who was worshipped by every woman on campus. He was on in years and had a witty and wise way about him. People feared him as much as they loved him. No one would ever have dared to say a word about him. It was not quite obvious that he preferred men. Most probably, he had never expressed it. He was too tasteful and he spent most of his time with families. He traveled with Beatrice and her husband. He loved taking tea with Elizabeth and having spirited political discussions with Mary. He avoided me for the longest time but he finally did come towards me and even pretended that we should travel together to Europe some time, to enjoy some gastronomy. I hero worshipped him from afar.

There we were. Late afternoon tea chez Beatrice. What would be the subject of the gathering? There certainly must be a reason for all this eminence late in the afternoon. Beatrice served tea and crumpets and Carolyn helped her distribute the munificence. We were all having such a good time that we forgot that we must really be there for some reason. Doubtless, someone besides Beatrice knew about the reasons why.

Beatrice disappeared for a moment and then reappeared with a book under her arm. Silence reigned as we realized that announcement time was near. Beatrice began: "My dear friends, we are gathered here today for a genuine reason. I thought you would like to know that our august campus has been invaded by a Judas, who has written a *roman-à-clef* about us which maligns a great number of us."

"Do they name names?"

"Not exactly. It is a *roman-à-clef*, after all, and someone of us will recognize ourselves and others and some will not."

"Why should that be a source of annoyance?" asked Edward Wallace. "It's par for the course, is it not?"

"Yes," Beatrice proffered, "but it could bring down a few marriages and relationships, and as such I do believe it is potentially dangerous."

"We're so close knit, we can fight fire with fire," Barlow added.

"Are you about to reveal the name of the culprit?" asked Elizabeth Schoen.

"Yes, I will."

"Is it one of us?" asked Carolyn conspiratorially.

"No, of course not," Beatrice answered. "I wouldn't have invited such a person to this tea."

"Well then," said Elspeth. "Just tell us and we'll boycott them."

"They could be run out of town," suggested Johann.

"Not so simple," Beatrice answered. "They're rather prestigious."

"Do they need the publicity?" I asked.

"I should think not," Beatrice said. "But they have some nerve to perpetrate such behavior."

"Do we have enough copies to go around?" asked Barlow. "We could all read it and then see what action to take based on the nefariousness of it all. We must try to be objective."

"Can one ever be objective about what attacks us?" asked Elizabeth.

Ann insisted: "Tell us who it is."

Beatrice answered, still cryptic. "You know them and you like them."

"Not any more, obviously." Ann was lugubrious, as she usually was.

"Will anyone lose tenure?" asked Johann.

"I doubt it," said Beatrice. "But it could explode a few happy relationships."

"If a relationship is truly happy, nothing can explode it. Gossip doesn't kill genuine relationships," added Edward Wallace.

Beatrice sat down, feeling slightly let down, as if she had done something foolish.

"Just tell us who it is," entreated Mary. "Then we'll see if we want to do anything drastic."

"It's the wife of our distinguished professor."

"The bitch!" shouted Carolyn. "I knew it. She had too much time on her hands. She has no courses to teach, no children to raise. What else could she do? She loves to compete with her distinguished husband. She probably thought she could earn a good bit with a revealing novel at about life on a small American campus. What an opportunity!"

"Any one of us might have done it if we were outsiders. She isn't really one of us. We were just fair game."

"Is it entertaining?" asked Elizabeth. "I can forgive it if it's entertaining. So few things ever are."

"It's what some of you would call a good read. But it's highly destructive and I'm afraid it will cause some real disasters among the people we know."

"Don't jump to conclusions, Beatrice. It may just be interesting for a few weeks and then everyone will get over it and it will be last year's sensation," said Paul Barlow.

"And last year's sensation is never very interesting this year. Especially on campus," added Ann, ever sure of herself.

"Which ones of us are in danger?" asked June.

Beatrice answered: "I'm not sure. But I certainly am."

That left a hole in the conversation. We wondered which one of Beatrice's infidelities was being discussed. I didn't blame her for being angry. There were stupid infidelities and there were deserved ones. Beatrice only deserved compassion. I understood her anger. Perhaps we could prevent her husband from reading the book.

"We could burn all the copies," I suggested, winking to Beatrice.

"This reminds me a bit of *Kristallnacht*" said Elizabeth. "I certainly hope there is no anti-Semitism in it."

"I never thought of that," said Carolyn. "You never know with these highfalutin novelists from the British empire. Anything is grist for their mill."

"Now let's not let ourselves go over the top. Let's just work out a secret plan to get rid of the perpetrator," said Barlow, ever the conspirator.

"How long do distinguished professorships last?" asked Ann.

"That depends on the president. He appoints them as he goes along," added Mary.

"Well then, our way is clear. Someone has to get to the president to suggest a new distinguished professorship. Mustn't keep them too long, must we?" winked Barlow.

"But the damage will be done quickly. We all have time to read, especially if it's something dangerous and damaging," pleaded Beatrice.

"I'm afraid you don't have too much good to say about academics," laughed Edward Wallace.

"It's the end of the season and none of us have time to waste before finals and the graduation," said Johann. "Probably no one will be able to get to it until after the semester."

"Bravo!" said Barlow.

"Many of us stay up all night if need be," added Beatrice, ever knowledgeable. "We haven't a moment to waste."

"Shall we draw up a list of the order of reading. We should simply pass the book around and not contribute to her vicious royalties," added economy-minded Carolyn.

"I have a piece of paper here. You may all sign and I will see to it that we each read it quickly. I'll phone you all," said Beatrice.

"How long do we have to read it. How many pages? I don't read very fast in English," said Elizabeth.

"Someone should make a list of the pages which concern each person," said Barlow.

"How would I know?" Beatrice pleaded. "I know what concerns me but I certainly don't know about many of the other allusions."

"Perhaps they are simply made up. How could she have done such effective research?" added June.

"And some of us are innocent," added Mary.

"Did you call just us because we're the ones in danger?" I asked.

"No, no," Beatrice insisted. "I just called my favorite people."

"What a relief!" Barlow added, cleverly. "I thought we were all at risk."

"Let's not get carried away," said Edward Wallace, ever civilized. "Let's just sign up and then go our merry ways."

We began to line up and we signed quietly. It was as if we were all trying to escape Big Brother and save our collective as well as individual reputations.

"This may very well be the most dramatic day I've ever lived through on this campus. I thought we had said goodbye to such things when Helmut and I left Vienna. But one is never safe, is one?" asked Elizabeth.

"Never," said Ann. "If you study history, all we do is go from bad to worse."

"What will your husband say to all this?" asked Mary.

"He'll probably just get drunk. That's his answer to everything," Ann proclaimed.

"Well, my friends," said Edward Wallace. "When shall we troubled souls meet again?"

"Tell us when that should be, Beatrice," said Mary.

"And we should probably meet somewhere else next time," said June. "We don't want them to trace where we meet too easily."

We agreed to meet as soon as enough of us had reported back to Beatrice. Meanwhile, one of us would have to be delegated to bring subtle pressure on the president. Someone who dined with him regularly.

"I'll do that", said Ann. "We have dinner every two weeks. I'll figure something out, you can trust me."

Everybody filed past Beatrice, hugging and kissing her. She didn't look any happier than she did before. Her husband walked in as we were filing out. We looked just a bit too conspiratorial. What would she tell him? I would have to ask her one day.

I walked back to my home and sat down with an iced vodka. I was already frightened that I might be among the people denounced and revealed. But something told me that this woman had not investigated me. But perhaps she had sources. You simply never knew.

Chapter Seventeen

Don looked penitent. It was early Sunday morning, we had finished breakfast and he was particularly non-loquacious. I decided to wait a moment before requesting to be enlightened about his mood. He had evinced an interest in spending the day painting and I thought I might make up final exams.

His mood was just as penitent about a half-hour later.

"Well, tell me what it is."

"What is what?"

It always took a careful cross-examination before I could come to some definite point of view. It was as if his moods changed like the weather. It might be expected to rain but sometimes the rain never expressed itself; sometimes there was quite a thunderstorm. One would always have to wait and see.

"Would you indulge me? I have a favor to ask of you."

"Your wish is my command."

"You're so gallant."

"Do you want to take a drive? Shall we abandon our resolves?"

"No. But would you... could you... go to church with me?"

"How lovely. I didn't know you went to church."

"My family does. And sometimes I miss the silliness of it."

"Which church do you go to?"

"It's high church. Episcopalian. The Anglo-Saxon answer to Catholicism. The church doesn't matter. It's the experience."

"That's fine, if you'll guide me."

"Don't you ever go?"

"I was brought up half-Jewish, half-Christian Scientist, and my family wasn't religious."

"Christian Scientist?"

"Yes. They don't believe in illness. When I was sick, my father's sisters would sing hymns to me on the telephone, which infuriated my mother."

"Maybe it's not a good idea. I just wanted to be in a sacrosanct atmosphere with you."

"Do you think we've made love too often? Are you feeling guilty?"

"Nothing so silly as that. I just want to know how it feels to be in the presence of God with you."

"God exists outside of churches, even in people's hearts."

"Don't be snide. I just wanted to hold your hand in church."

"That's a tall order, Don. I'll have to bring a coat or a scarf so we won't be discovered."

"Don't worry. We'll find a secluded place where we won't be seen."

"You need a pretty big church for that."

"Maybe it's a bad idea."

"No. Actually, I like it. You just never cease to surprise me with the dimensions of your personality."

"I go into things deeply."

"You certainly do."

"We have to be there on time, early even, so that we can find the right place."

"Just tell me when and where we go."

"There's a lovely church I used to go to when I first arrived in town. We can walk from here. You'll see. It will be very pleasant."

"I know. I'm looking forward to it."

He came over to me, held my face in his hands and kissed me on the forehead. I kissed him on his eyelids.

"Don't do that. You'll excite me and then I won't be in any condition to go."

We walked down to the rather imposing church of the holy sacrament. We walked up the stairs and I secretly hoped we would meet no one in particular. Most of my friends at the college were non-practicing anything and so it didn't seem likely. Those who partied Saturday night were rarely over their hangovers on early Sunday. We sat down at the back, on the side, two little orphans of the storm, and awaited the beginning of the service. The organ music was particularly enchanting and I resolved to come more often, if only to calm myself. Ever since Beatrice's tea party, I had been particularly nervous. I kept praying that all would be well and that she was needlessly anguished. Every time the phone rang, my heart skipped a beat.

Don spread a rather imposing scarf over our laps. Then he placed his hand underneath it. I did the same and we were sitting there holding hands like two little lovebirds. I didn't dare look at him because I was afraid one of us would burst out laughing. And it probably would not be him.

He squeezed my hand. "I wish I could marry you. Then I would truly be happy."

"It's being done."

"It is?"

"Yes, some of the lunatic fringe are doing it. But the publicity is not very positive."

"I certainly understand it. If it's forever, it should be consecrated."

"Yes, but you don't even know if it's till next season."

"I know."

"Yes, but you want to make everything ultimate. I feel like it's a scene from *Madame Bovary*."

"It's so much easier to be literary. It takes the onus off it."

"We have to learn how to behave. Let's just be very quiet and breathe the wonderful atmosphere."

"Fine idea."

The service began and it was indeed in the best of taste. I was afloat on a sea of religious feeling and I was deeply happy. Don squeezed my hand and once he even tickled my palm. I refused to give in to his natural mischievousness. I would try to keep him on the straight and narrow track. If he wanted to feel together in this way, he should experience this feeling. I was experiencing it, certainly. At one point, the reverend was speaking in a rather sensual manner. His sermon consisted of finding God in the simplest everyday things. It was a simple, lovely homily. When he said everyday things for about the third time, Don moved his hand away and took hold of my crotch. When I looked at him in horror, he winked and said: "Everyday things."

For the rest of the sermon, he held steadfastly to my private parts and I was shocked that I never even got an erection. He probably did. I wanted to hit his hands but I realized that it was too much of a protest. If this was what he wanted, he would have it. After all, it was he who thought of all this. He would have to live with his desire. I just hoped he would not get down on his knees to worship. I shut my eyes and suddenly I was in the movie house and experiencing the delicious terror of that moment.

When the sermon was over and people started to rise, we did not move. We were both so lost in our experience that I felt we could spend the rest of the day there, experiencing this epiphany.

When we finally got ourselves together and I stopped blushing, we walked slowly out, not looking at one another. All of a sudden I saw the lady who had perpetrated the book, on the arm of her very distinguished husband. How could I get out of there without her seeing me? It was not of very great importance. It was hardly possible for her to publish a sequel in the next few weeks. Who could know how prolific she was? She would surely not try the same literary shenanigans a second time. No one would be that stupid or vicious, or would they?

We walked quietly towards home and still did not converse. I decided not to tell Don about what happened at Beatrice's place. He might be particularly upset by it and I didn't wish to precipitate any withdrawal feelings. Now that we were illegally married, it would be better to preserve each other's good feelings. One had to protect one's spouse. Was Don what I would have sought to marry?

Perhaps not. I always wanted a woman like Anne, a woman of the world, cultured, creative, of another social maelstrom. But that was perhaps also nothing but foolishness. I could never belong to certain worlds. Her world would surely reject me. I didn't have the requisite money. I didn't have the requisite inheritance or position. Or did that matter?

Don must have come from a moneyed bourgeois world as well. He would never reveal it. But he came from family that was proud of itself. He found what we were up to strangely frightening. He wanted to espouse it totally. but he was constantly aware that it was not what his future potentially was. He had found his love but not his way. I wasn't what he thought I was. If he ever disconnected with me sexually, he would be free to find another life. I was so permissive with him that he did not wish to rebel against me. If he had known what I had done with Peter, he might have been disgusted, but a part of him would have understood. Who knows what he had done before me? Had I really introduced him to this life, or did he know it peripherally before? I could never ask such questions. I would only go along with what had transpired. I would be the answer to his present prayer, in church or out.

When we arrived at the house, he took my hand and thanked me. "*Mille grazie, caro mio.*"

"Say it in French."

"I'd rather not. I'd make a mistake."

"Won't you come up and spend the day? Now that we're married, I mean."

"I can't. If I do that, I won't get anything done and neither will you."

"You're usually right. I bow to your superior wisdom."

"Good. Have a wonderful afternoon."

"When shall we see each other?"

"Pick me up at the end of the afternoon and we'll go have a pizza."

I laughed, he laughed. "Do you know of another place?"

"No need to find another place. He was put in his place. He won't try that again."

"Unless that's what you're hoping for. You always had a penchant for a *ménage à trois*."

"Not really. I'm just an experimenter, like our friend Anne."

"Well then, I'll see you later."

He blew me a kiss and walked off into the sunlight.

Chapter Eighteen

I sat there making up exams, consulting notes, feeling virtuous, even religious. The phone rang and I seriously considered not answering it. But, of course, I did. I'd have to get one of those answering services one of these days. There were real reasons for those things.

It was Peter. I knew it would have to be Peter. He had an uncanny ability to smell his moment.

"Hi, teach. How are you doing?"

"I'm doing."

"What are you doing?"

"I'm making up exams."

"Would you like me to be a guinea pig?"

"We've already done that."

"You were the guinea pig."

"That's what I'm afraid of."

"Don't you want to prepare me for the final."

"You mean you want to see it so you can bone up."

"I wasn't suggesting that. I just want to be prepared. Try me."

"I've already done that."

"Do you think I'm passing material?"

"I think you're A #1."

"I feel flattered."

"You feel proud of yourself."

"Peter, this comedy cannot go on. *La commedia è finita.*"

"That sounds like something I've heard before."

"Try the opera *Pagliacci*."

"I saw that once. Hot stuff."

"For you, Peter, everything is hot stuff."

"Everything to do with you."

"Where are you, Peter?"

"Around the corner."

"I'll give you one hour, Peter. And we will study for the exams. We might as well get it done. But one false move and out you go."

"You're great. You're nonpareil."

"You're a fucking menace."

"Can I bring something?"

"Just bring yourself, as they say."

"I'll be right there."

I felt remiss, terrible, and yet somehow relieved. This morning in church was a bit much for me. Peter was a fine antidote to Don. After seeing Don, I wanted to cry. After seeing Peter, I could laugh. It reminded me of part of the sermon. 'Life is a tragedy for those who feel. It is a comedy for those who think.' Don had squeezed me tight when he used the word 'feel'. I wondered whether I had not been given Peter as an antidote to Don and vice versa. It was unkind to think this, but life's juxtapositions were fascinating. Anne was also an antidote. Everyone was an antidote for everyone else.

Peter bounded up the stairs and before I knew it was upon me. His ample body filled the room with its athletic perfume. He was totally in love with himself. He filled every atmosphere with his limitless self-confidence. I thought of smelling his underarm odor. It would some day have to be bottled. *Eau de Pierre*. Lucky, lucky Pierre.

"Hi, Teach. You have an exam for me?"

"As a matter of fact, I do." I stuck a piece of paper in front of his nose. It was last term's exam and he would certainly have immense difficulties with it.

"May I consult my dictionary?"

"Certainly not."

"But that could help."

"It could also harm. Most people do not know how to use a dictionary."

"Use or abuse."

"Shut up and take a look at this. Then you'll understand what you're up against."

"It makes me hot with intellectual desire."

"You're the only student turned on by an exam."

"By the teacher who made up the exam."

"What a distinction."

"There is one."

"Peter, you only have an hour."

"That doesn't give me enough time."

"Oh yes it does, enough time to figure out what you don't know. It will liberate you."

"Yes, but that won't give me time to get rid of my erection."

"That you can do at home. While you realize how frustrated you are."

"You're trying to hurt me."

"That's what you did to me last time."

"I didn't hurt you. I pleasured you."

"Incidentally."

"Yes. I did my honest, level best. Maybe that wasn't your position. Maybe you'd like to do something else."

"I'm not taking the exam Peter, you are."

"That depends."

He sat there for a moment or two, realizing that what I said was true. He took out a cigarette and lit it, offering me one.

"I don't smoke."

"You have all the virtues."

After another few moments, he stood up. His enormous erection was more than visible.

"Frustration time, eh?"

He came up to me and I heard him whisper: "Please."

He took his enormous member out of its encasing and pushed me down into my chair. Before I knew it, he was touching it to my lips.

"Take me, fella."

I obeyed.

Chapter Nineteen

I quit working around five and decided to find Don. I was exhausted inside of myself, wondering where we would go from here. As I was about to leave, the phone rang. It was Beatrice.

"Hello, my dear. Thank you for your moral support the other day."

"I was worried for you."

"I felt I had to go public with all this. Ann called to say she and her husband were working on the president to bring in a new distinguished professor in English literature. He also said he didn't think they would wish to stay beyond this semester. He was waiting to hear from them."

"Good. Everything in its own good time. Some day all this potential panic won't matter. Some day people will be free to go their own way."

"Do you think so, dear? I don't. Certain things will always be taboo."

"How can we keep living without any freedom?"

"Certain kinds of freedom are harmful to certain people. And there is human pride and human prejudice."

"You sound like a British novel, Beatrice dear."

"I really called to tell you that it's your turn for the book if you still want to read it."

"Of course. I can't wait. How do I pick it up?"

"Either you come by my place some time in the next twenty-four hours or I'll come to you."

I didn't wish her to be involved with Don. "Am I ruining the schedule if I meet you tomorrow?"

"No, certainly not, unless you could read it tonight. But I haven't given you enough time to prepare."

"Unfortunately I'm out to dinner this evening."

"I could leave it in your mailbox."

"That would be fine. Can you do it in the next few hours?"

"Of course. I'll just walk over."

"Beatrice, is it fair to ask? Is there something in there about me?"

"My dear, I wouldn't know. There is about me."

"Well, that's why you got started with all this. But perhaps it will be like so many *romans-à-clef*, interesting for a moment and then not any more."

"If my husband reads it, our marriage is over."

"Why? He's no fool."

"Our marriage has been over for some time. So many things end before they end. And then all that is needed is something to set everything off."

"If people are waiting for excuses, they can use anything."

"That's certainly true. I'm just not ready to allow my marriage to disintegrate while our son is only in his early teens. I need to wait."

"I can understand. Can I help?"

"Yes, just read the book and tell me what you think."

"Has Paul read it?"

"Yes, he was the first."

"What does he think?"

"That it's badly written. He called it a potboiler. He was very annoyed."

"Style is very important. A book which is well written is more lethal than one which is not."

"I wouldn't know about style in English. But the content is lethal."

"Well then, dear, leave the book for me and I'll try to digest it quickly. Fortunately, I've made up my exams so I can do the reading on schedule. But I don't want it to ruin my dinner this evening."

"When you return, it will be in an envelope addressed to you in your mailbox. Fortunately, it's not a very huge book. It can be read in a few hours."

"You'll hear from me soon. *Bon courage*, Beatrice."

"I thank you."

I hurried to get out of the house before there was another call. I drove over to Don's cubby hole. There he was, lost in thought, contemplating his navel.

"I thought you'd never come."

"I had a call just before I left. One of my friends asked me to read a book and discuss it with her."

"The imperatives of the academic life."

"It's nice to know we have the freedom to read."

"And the freedom to write."

"And the freedom to express ourselves."

"And the freedom to hide it all from those who might bad mouth us."

"One day even that might be a thing of the past."

"I doubt people will ever stop maligning each other."

"Be of good cheer."

"Small campuses, like small places, breed the worst forms of maligning. Nothing is worse than the small-time mentality."

"I thought academia was filled with great minds."

"Sometimes. And great minds often harbor great meanness. Academics are not the most exemplary people."

"Then why do you bother to live in this atmosphere?"

"Because I love teaching. Students are wonderful."

"There's probably just as much meanness among them as in any part of the academic life."

"You're probably right. But I think I prefer artists and creative people to limited academics."

"Why should academics be limited?"

"Because they know more and more about less and less."

"It's better than knowing less and less about more and more."

"You're very funny."

"I try to be."

"I hope some day you'll be an academic, too."

"I don't. I just want a simple nine to five existence."

"What about your art, your creation?"

"I wouldn't want it if it didn't bring me honor and success, and I seriously doubt I have the makings of an important artist."

"You're too cruel to yourself."

"I have a certain lucidity. You have the makings of an artist."

"How do you know?"

"Because you care."

"Care?"

"Caring is the key to it all."

"I thought technique and know-how were."

"Caring makes it all happen."

"I hope you write a book some day which tells us all how to use that caring."

"Perhaps I will. Perhaps I won't. I don't care enough."

"Don't you care about anything?"

"Yes, I do. Right now I care about you. And right now I care about us. And I care to go eat something."

"Will it be pizza?"

"Why not. We both like it and it's relaxed."

"If that guy puts the make on us again, I might just get heartburn."

"Why?"

"I have too much on my plate."

"He won't dare. And if he does, it will be a hoot."

"There you go again. You're curious."

"Of course I'm curious. Curiosity is what makes the world go round."

"And curiosity killed the cat."

"We all have to go sometime."

"You're outrageous."

"I suppose I am. If my curiosity were to go, I wouldn't have anything."

"What if I start boring you? If your curiosity about me were to end, would that be the end of us?"

"Perhaps. But I think I will be curious about you to the end of my days."

"I certainly hope so."

We drove over to the pizza place and found a table. Our friend was on duty, twirling and creating his magnificent creations. He didn't notice us right away. Perhaps we could keep a low profile.

Don admired his skill. "I don't know how he does it. He's a magician with that dough."

"Maybe that's what you should do, ultimately. Make those fabulous pizzas."

"I wouldn't mind. But once again, I might be sated with it all in a few weeks. Then what would I do?"

"You could do research on pizza technique. There must be various ways to do it. In southern France, the pizzas are deliciously thin. There are so many ways to make them."

"You see. There will always be something new. We could travel through France and Italy to research the subject."

"We'd become food writers. I can see our book. *The Pizza Phenomenon*."

"Why don't we do that this summer?"

"Would you like to? Would you like to spend the summer together in Europe?"

"I certainly would. But I have to go home to the family for a while and then see how much money I had."

"I could take you. I could manage it. Pizza doesn't cost much, after all."

"But we won't be able to eat just that. If we did, we'd become enormous."

"Not if we skipped meals."

"After all, we could basically live on love. A loaf of bread, a jug of wine..."

"And lots of pizza."

We were sighted. He looked over at us and then went back to his virtuosity. The waitress came over to us and we ordered extravagantly. But first we guzzled beer.

"We could study the beer situation, as well."

"I understand the Belgians have more different kinds of beer than any of the other countries. There's even one called *la mort subite*, with the flavor of berries."

"Sudden death with berries. How romantic."

"I'm more excited about going to Europe with you than anything else. Please don't forget that. Even if it's a short trip. I want to show you Paris and Rome, and who knows."

Our pizza maker was staring at us every time he got a moment. He looked very disillusioned. Annoyed.

"I think he's not very happy with us."

"So what. We're only customers."

"Don, suddenly I feel very happy. I wondered what would happen after this semester, after you graduated, after you went your way. I knew I couldn't lure you to New York, but we could try Europe. Perhaps we could settle down there."

"We'll see. First we have to get through the next month or so."

"We will."

"One day at a time."

"That's the watchword for alcoholics."

"They're a bright bunch. They miss the joys of alcohol, but they have the joy of living."

We devoured our gorgeous pizzas as soon as they were brought. I made a toast with a glass of beer. "Here's to Europe."

"Here's to Europe."

Our pizza maker saw us clinking glasses and couldn't stop concentrating on us. After we paid our bill, Don insisted on going over to speak to him.

"Great, as ever. You're a talented man."

"Thank you." He was as solemn as he could be.

I added: "We admire your talent. Where did you learn to do this?"

"In Italy."

"Where in Italy?"

"Napoli."

"The center of it all," I said, trying to seem knowledgeable.

Don connected with him more and more. "What's your name?"

"Antonio."

"Bravo, Antonio."

"Why don't you want to see me?"

"We're afraid," Don said, like a little boy.

"Afraid of what?"

"You're so manly."

"Why does that make you afraid?"

"We don't know what you would do to us."

"Are you afraid of my pizzas?"

"No."

"Napoli is supposed to be a dangerous city," I articulated.

"I only grew up there. Every place is dangerous... a little."

I wondered what Beatrice would say to that. She had probably never descended to a pizza meal. Or perhaps she had, with her son.

"I want to spend some time with you. After all, you are two and I am only one. Maybe you are dangerous."

He had a point. Don asked the crucial question: "When do you get off tonight?"

"In half an hour."

I took Don aside. "Look. Why don't you go out drinking with him? I have some things I have to do. This is more to your taste than to mine."

"I want to bring him back to your place."

"Why?"

"I think it's all part of the curiosity. We need to have more experience."

I was angry, yet I would have done anything rather than read Beatrice's book. I decided to be forgiving. "Do whatever you like. Shall we wait for him?"

We did. We waited out in the car and Antonio joined us shortly. He had a car, as well and we decided he should follow us in his.

"We're both riding in Buick convertibles. That must mean we have something in common."

More laughing. Then we were off. In just a few minutes, we were parking nearby my house. I went over to the mailbox and the promised package was there. Don admired it: "You always have mail, my friend. You're never forgotten for one moment."

Antonio followed us up the stairs and in a few minutes, we were quite *gemütlich*. We were drinking beers and sitting listening to the Brando record. We decided, without consulting, to quiz him about his young life. He was twenty-four, he had been making pizzas since he was knee high to a grasshopper and he and his family had come here from Napoli a few years ago. He wanted to go to school but he had to stash away some money before he could do that. He was obviously impressed by our connection with the university. He asked no questions. His coal black eyes told their own story. After a while, he asked to use the john.

We stared at each other as he entered it. He was rather diminutive, no more than five six, surely. He was compact and he moved like a puma or a leopard. He was more embarrassed than we were.

"Shall I leave him to you? Try him out and call me later if it's worth it."

"No. Either both of us or not at all. That's what's turning him on."

"Do you think he likes girls?"

"He certainly does. He reminds me of me. He wants to try everything before he gets married."

"What if he likes what he tries and wants a *ménage à trois*?" I asked.

"No chance. He just wants to see what it's all about. And we could hire him to teach us how to make pizzas. We could say that was why we brought him home."

"Do you think he'd go for that?"

"He might. We could reward him with a little money and a little sex."

"You're really quite ingenious."

"I don't know. All I know is I'm having so much fun with it."

"I feel like I'm part of an archeological pizza dig."

"Probably nobody has ever done it before."

Our friend came back and sat down dutifully, uncertain as to the next move. He didn't have the audacity of either Don or Peter. Peter could have undone him in two shakes of a lamb's tail, or something to that effect.

Don decided to go all out: "We want to learn how to make pizzas."

Antonio laughed. "Then you can not need me any more."

"We want to imitate you."

"But you cannot do it quickly. And you don't have the ovens."

"But will you show us how to do it?"

"Yes, yes. If you come to the pizza place on an off hour, I will show you. It cannot be done anywhere else."

"Good idea."

"It would be an honor to show you but not many people have the ability. You are very surprising to me." He laughed.

"What could we do for you?" Don pursued, more and more wicked.

"You could teach me about your life. You could show me something of it."

"What part of it?"

He was very shy and very circumspect. "Whatever you wish to. I think you know. You are not a little boy."

The three of us sat contemplating one another. Don distributed more beers. As he handed Antonio his, Antonio took hold of his arm in a masterly fashion. Antonio pulled him down to his knees and they contemplated one another strongly. Don looked slightly frightened. I was not sure what to do. Antonio took Don's head in his hands and stared into his eyes. Don was obviously thrilled by the strength of it all. I was rather frightened. Antonio let him go and got up. Don stretched out his hands and placed them firmly on Antonio's buttocks. Antonio froze, as if turning into a statue.

"Remove my clothes."

Now the ritual began. Don slowly did just that and we contemplated a small replica of the David. Had anyone ever been formed so perfectly? So svelte, so harmonious. Don held him in his arms and kissed him quietly. I couldn't move. Antonio's eyes beckoned me and he formed his lips into a moue. Don held out his hand to me. I arrived and stood in back of Antonio, up against the perfection of this Italian statue. We were both taller than he was. His clothes were at his feet.

Don picked them up and we led him down the familiar corridor. His erect penis was sculptured, pink and rosy. His exquisitely formed body was crowned by this magnificent appendage. There was nothing at the Metropolitan Museum to equal it. Was there anything in Florence more enticing? We took turns embracing him on the mouth. He was not experienced in any way and that made it even more delightful. He was a virgin with men and I hoped he would not despise us for these acts. I would have preferred to watch. I wanted to be a voyeur. Don would not let me. He was so moved by our lovemaking that he soon ejaculated. But that was the only beginning. He was more and more insistent on contact. He lay down on me and we did the missionary position, as if I were a girl. Don enveloped us like a human sandwich and brought us both to climax with his tongue.

When it was all over, we lay there gasping. Antonio dressed first, quietly and in orderly fashion. He looked at us and gave his orders: "I will expect you for your first lesson in pizza making Wednesday afternoon at three. Thank you, gentleman, for your lesson in lovemaking. Ciao."

We sat there in the half darkness and wondered at the mysteries of the human body. I tried not to fall asleep. I had to stay awake and read that book. Don fell asleep almost immediately. I made a pot of coffee and took the novel out of its container. I read all night long, consuming huge amounts of coffee. I felt like Honoré de Balzac, only I wasn't writing the work at hand. When I read the last line towards dawn, I realized what it was to conceive a work which was a *roman-à-clef*. How had she done it? Was it perpetrated out of hate or just out of boredom? I tried to think who was who but it wasn't easy to do so. I was obviously not one of the characters. That was a relief but the subject of homosexuality was not neglected. It was part and parcel of the entire volume. There were a network of literary homosexuals and the young men they stalked. The age difference was played upon mightily.

It was surely Paul Barlow and Edward Wallace, and even Johann, the social womanizer. She had caught it all. But she did not name names. Poor Beatrice. Her husband was unfaithful to her with a number of younger ladies. And she was busy sleeping with quite a few men to give them solace in their difficult lives. She was, as in her real life, an enabler, a kind woman who helped men when they were betrayed by their errant spouses. How did this British literary harridan find out so much? It was research like anything else. And perhaps quite a bit of conjecture, as well. Fortunately, literature was not life. It was the essence of life. It was the elixir of life. It was what Picasso and Cocteau had said it was: art was a lie which told the truth. Plato had been right. Poets were liars. But he was wrong: they suggested a deeper truth. Could I ever perpetrate such a novel? Perhaps it was Don in his infinite curiosity who would one day do it. Balzac did it. Dickens did it. Proust did it. It was an art brought about by deep necessity. How else could the truth be known?

Chapter Twenty

Beatrice answered in her usual cautious manner. "I did it. I read it all."

"Did you enjoy it?"

"Yes, I suppose. I can see why you hate it."

"Aram has already read it. It's an armed camp at my house, as I thought it would be."

"I'm so sorry."

"Can't you just deny it all?"

"What's the point of it?"

"You're both implicated."

"What's good for the goose..."

"Should be good for the gander."

"What shall I do with the book?"

"Would you bring it to Elizabeth? She's expecting it."

"Fine. Shall I call her?"

"Just to find out her schedule."

"I will dear. Remember, we love you."

"Too many of you do."

"I'll be in touch. If he does anything terrible, let me know. I'll take you to dinner."

"Take me to dinner if he doesn't do anything terrible."

"I'll call Elizabeth."

Beatrice trailed off and the next voice was Elizabeth.

"Elizabeth dear, I have the fateful novel to bring to you."

"I have been informed. Do drop it over at your convenience. Helmut and I are meditating what we shall do with it."

"I can bring it by in an hour."

"Good. I intend to read it to him over some left-over sauerkraut."

"How appropriate."

"Is it worth noodles, do you think?"

"I think the sauerkraut is just the thing."

"Beer or coffee?"

"It's not soporific. Just guessing who is who takes a little doing."

"I hope Helmut and I are not implicated. I understand we are the only faithful couple on campus."

"I didn't know you were that dull."

"Darling, we were never dull. If we set out to be unfaithful, no one would ever know."

"I'm glad to hear it."

"You know, young man, you do have a Hungarian temperament."

"How do you know?"

"We're Viennese. They're the only ones who understand the other part of the empire."

"I'll bring you your book forthwith."

"You're welcome to stay for some sauerkraut."

"Then you won't have time to read."

"You could tell us about it and save us the effort."

"I see you prefer art and music to literature."

"I didn't know it was literature. I thought it was pornography."

"Not quite."

"Then why should we bother?" She gave off one of her wonderful devious horse-laughs. We were very fortunate to have this delicious couple on campus. All the foreigners were more fun than the native Americans.

"Auf wiederschauen."

"Not if I see you first."

After I dropped off the novel, I started walking toward my office. I would run off the exams. One had to be prepared ahead of time for any contingency. On the way to Boylan Hall, I ran into Paul.

"There's the man of the hour. I understand you spent the night reading our *roman-à-clef*."

"News travels fast."

"Well, what do you think?"

"It will never win the Nobel prize."

"With what is getting it these days, it just might."

"What do you think we should do? Shall we challenge them to a duel?"

"I'd like to do something to her. But there are laws against it."

"You know there's going to be a lecture by him at the Honors College this week. I think that if we all went, we could confront her in some meaningful way."

"Do you think she'd have the nerve to show up?"

"Certainly, if her redoubtable husband is giving a lecture. We could make some mischief."

"Well, I'm game if you need me."

"I'll be in touch."

"Just give me an evening or so."

"Oh yes, we're busy right now with our undergraduates."

"Roy, I hope you're not writing a novel."

"As a matter of fact I am, but nothing about this formidable place."

"Well then, just call."

I walked on to my office and found Peter waiting for me.

"Peter, don't you ever have time to study?"

"Hi, teach. I've already done my studying for the day."

"Good, then maybe they need you at the gymnasium."

"I thought I'd bone up on my French."

"You mean French up on your bone."

"You're trying to be vulgar. I'm the one who's vulgar, remember?"

"I really don't know which one of us is the most vulgar."

We entered my office and Peter sat down before I did.

"You act as if you own this place."

"I'm just tuckered out from all the work I've done. You've worn me out."

"Peter, don't you have anything better to do with your time?"

"Yes and no."

"You're going to pass the course, I'm sure. You don't have to put forth any more effort. You've done it already."

"*Merci, professeur.*"

"You see, you're starting to think in French. I knew it would happen."

"*Baise-moi.*"

"You've got to learn a few more expressions, my boy."

"*Voulez-vous coucher avec moi?*"

"Something less rudimentary."

"*Je t'aime, je t'adore, que veux-tu encore?*"

"Where did you learn that?"

"I bought a phrase book."

"I hope they never let you loose in France."

"I'm going there for my honeymoon some day."

"I'd learn a few more expressions if I were you."

"I will. *Donnez-moi le fromage.*"

"That's more like it, Peter. That will get you far."

"J'aime beaucoup le professeur."

"You have a one track mind."

"Le professeur me baise beaucoup."

"I wouldn't admit it if I were you."

"Le professeur est si gentil."

"If you keep this up, you'll become a French major."

"I would have if I had started earlier."

"Well, one never knows. You could stay on."

"Just give me a good college hug."

"And just what does that mean?"

"Make me feel like I'm a good guy. I really care."

"What do I have to do to get liberated?"

"Just pleasure me a little."

"Tu es un bon garçon."

He came over and hugged me until I hurt. He waited for me to get excited. I refused to pleasure him.

"You got up on the wrong side of the bed, as they say."

"I spent the whole night up and I'm tired."

"I didn't know I had that much of an effect on you."

"I was reading a book."

"You intellectuals. You never know when to stop."

"There you're accurate. We never do."

He began massaging my behind in the most insidious manner.

"Just drop your pants and I'll calm my little boy."

I tried to hit him.

"Don't do that again. That's not very nice."

"I swear. You have to know when to stop."

He got up, opened the door and slammed it behind him.

One up for me, the first time I had ever won with Peter. He looked so forlorn when he left. There were limits and he had reached them. Brute force was not my strong suit. I couldn't keep up with all of this. One day Peter would catapult out of my life and I wanted to retain my self-respect. I felt violated.

Chapter Twenty-One

I went home and decided to lock my door. I needed rest.

The phone rang, of course. It was Anne.

"Darling. What a surprise."

"You sound tired."

"I haven't slept all night. It's very hectic up here."

"New York is quiet these days, or else it just is my life that's not percolating."

"Have you been practicing?"

"Yes. I think *Carnaval* is ready."

"Great. Could you come up around graduation and give a recital?"

"Do you think I could?"

"Life isn't too short. We could use one more artist."

"I'd love to. It would be a privilege."

"Wonderful. I'll schedule it and call you. It should be a great moment."

"Will Don forgive you?"

"Of course. If he doesn't want to come, but I'm sure he will. Besides, everyone is in an uproar here. The wife of our distinguished professor has written a *roman-à-clef* and some of us are up to our ears in scandal. A recital will calm things down."

"Just let me know, my dear. I promise to be good."

"You don't need to be good. You have to be great."

Paul called and told us that the Honors College lecture was on Friday evening. We would see notices posted for a lecture on Vita Sackville-West and Harold Nicholson. It was an ideal choice.

We all showed and the audience was filled with the élite of the college. Madame the perpetrator was sitting in the front row. That woman certainly had a nerve. I sat next to Beatrice and Paul was on her other side so that we would be close to her in case there was a bad moment. Aram, of course, was too busy and was giving his own lecture at a nearby college campus.

Sigmund Nachman, the head of the Honors College, did the honors and we were treated to a most erudite speech about the scandals of another literary era. Elizabeth and Helmut were right in back of me and she leaned forward to give me a piece of her mind.

"My dear, you can't imagine what a piece of trash that was. It wouldn't translate into Viennese, I can tell you that. I wonder why people don't realize that sexual machinations are no more interesting than slipping on a banana peel."

"That's positively Bergsonian," I quipped.

"Such sleaze," Paul continued.

"We'll call it 'A slice of sleaze' for the paperback."

Our speaker went on despite all the little side commentaries and we were better behaved when Sig Nachman stared pointedly at our section. After the applause, we were asked to come to the banquet room for refreshments. We went en masse. There was punch and several hors d'oeuvres. We wondered silently whether a manifestation might be made. The solution came most apropos. Carolyn, who had a penchant for falling, which she had used brilliantly in *The Cherry Orchard*, was talking volubly and waving her punch glass as she spoke, as she was wont to do. Paul, taking advantage of the poor girl, purposely tripped her and she went skidding right into Mme novelist. The punch ruined her rather florid frock. It all happened in a moment. Our little group stared at the lady most meaningfully and quickly dispersed. Carolyn tried to apologize but we pulled her along so that it would not really look like an accident. We were in fine fettle.

"Masterful," proclaimed Elizabeth.

"*Un coup de génie*," said Helmut and we went walking along in a happy bunch. We ended up at Helmut and Elizabeth's where we were treated to more drinks and some wonderful Viennese pastries. I announced Anne's impending concert and everyone promised to come. Graduation was shaping up to be a splendid affair. We were positively joyous.

I went skipping back to the house and was happy to find that Don had already arrived. I was only worried that the advent of Anne might be disturbing to him.

I decided to broach it to him directly. No use making any allusions. I hadn't had a chance to ask him how his pizza lesson had gone. I couldn't make it of course. He would probably be feeling guilty and so I intended to capitalize on that guilt.

"How was your pizza lesson?"

"Cheesy," he replied.

"I know but did you learn anything?"

"Yes, I did. That guy had no intention of teaching me anything. He just tried to make me on the spot."

"Did you enjoy it *in medias res*?"

"I didn't enjoy it without you."

"Well, that's nice to know. Loyalty is always touching."

"Touching is not always loyalty. Anyway, he wants a threesome. One is not enough."

"The more toppings, the better, eh?"

"He's in the other room."

"I didn't give my permission."

"He brought pizza."

"Good. I'm hungry, after all the events of the evening."

"I told him you might not approve."

"I will if you hear me out. I have something to tell you."

"What is it?"

"I'm having a party for graduation. Anne will be coming up to play *Carnaval* for the folks. She was afraid you might disapprove. I told her you'd probably love it."

"You have me by the balls."

"No, it's our friend there that has us by the balls."

"If you object to Anne, I'll reject her but it was my idea and it seemed like a very festive way to end the season. We'll all be on a high and it will be like the summation of this very complicated season, if you know what I mean."

"We could serve a dozen types of pizza."

"I intend to do a few hors d'oeuvre, some shrimp."

"Not without Dana."

"There are other people who can shell and devein."

"We'll work something out."

I saw that Don was nervous about the presence of our Italian friend. I would try to make it easier for him. "Look, why don't you proceed to the lesson and I'll just sit here and contemplate my naval base."

"He wants you."

"I know, but I feel bad about it, having not had a lesson from him."

"Don't be a horse's ass."

"That's exactly what I don't want to be."

"You owe me this. We started together."

"I don't like sleeping with statues. He reminds me of the David. Once in Rome I met someone who was like the David. He was so beautiful, I couldn't even manage an erection. I just looked at him in awe.

"Maybe that's why he likes you. He doesn't turn you on. It's a challenge."

"He makes me feel inadequate."

"I don't believe that for a moment."

"Well then, tell him I'm here and I'm hungry and we can eat first."

"Good idea."

A moment later, the David entered. Antonio was in the altogether. I had never had a pizza served to me before by a statue. It was rather sweet and made me think I was back in Italy.

We all took off our clothes and sat down on the rug, drinking beers and eating the absolutely sensational pizza with a world of toppings. Something made me find it funny. I kept thinking of Carolyn falling all over the lady novelist. Life was suddenly delightfully amusing. After we ate and drank ourselves silly, we found ourselves wondering who would make the first move. Antonio removed the plates and the glasses and decided to do the dishes. We called him from the kitchen. He must not be servile.

"You men make me feel so happy in my new country."

"That's very nice, Antonio."

"We couldn't ask for anything more," Don proclaimed.

"I want to pleasure you. How can I do that?"

"You already have, Antonio."

"I mean... you know what I mean."

"You must be very quiet, Antonio and we will dance together to a lovely, slow tango."

Don put on the tango record. Antonio and I made the subtle movements and we danced on and on into the night. It was very late by the time we went down the corridor, arm in tendentious arm.

Chapter Twenty-Two

It was final exam time. Everyone was on the qui vive. I saved papers to grade during each one so that I wouldn't be spending all my time staring at them as they worked. There was an honor system on campus which was never to be forgotten. The students stood in judgment on their own fellow students. If someone were cheating, the teacher had no responsibility. Each of the students signed a voucher on each piece of work. It was so reassuring.

Don sat quietly writing. Occasionally, he would look up at me and through me. Once he even winked. I tried to remain stony faced throughout. Some of the students came up to communicate with me, some asked questions, a few went to the john. Don just sat there. There he was, my lover, my helpmate, my curiosity killed the cat mate, my partner in crime, my star of the season. I looked at him both subjectively and objectively, if such a thing could be imagined. The weather was warmer but he still wore a light sweater, this time a white cardigan, which somehow showed off his pensive face to great advantage. He looked more and more like the actor Fred McMurray. He had a splendid square jaw and worry wrinkles around his eyes. His thinning hair showed off his high forehead. His lower lip revealed his natural sensuality. I wondered what he would look like in thirty years. His lanky body was soft and supple in the most endearing fashion. It was impossible not to love him. It was impossible not to admire him.

Yet there was a stubborn streak in him which made me fearful. If he believed something, he would never veer away from his belief. He was, in his own way, non-corruptible. Where would he turn in life? Would he continue to paint and play music? Would he express himself? Would his somewhat religious bent and philosophical need turn him into a reliable bourgeois? Would he turn away from the life he was leading and become an insurance salesman, as he sometimes predicted? Could he lead his life with a man? Could he turn back to marriage and children as a way of existence, just to be part of a certain fabric of society? If he did that, he might one day revert again, once he had produced the children and lived the expected life. But that would be in many long years and by that time I would be a very old gentleman, indeed.

When the exam was over, he was one of the last to leave. In fact, he waited until all the others left to give me his blue books. He did not write a great deal. He drew me a few pictures and he just seemed to want to be alone with me for a pregnant moment.

"I tried to do good. Give me the grade I deserve. Don't play favorites. I tried to remember all the wonderful things you've taught me."

"I'm sure you did wonderfully well. How considerate of you. You touch me deeply."

"No more deeply than you touch me. I'm genuinely sad that I'll never have a chance to study formally with you again."

"We could do some project together."

"I'm sure we will. There's only one answer I was proud of. It was about Racine's *Bérénice*."

154

"Our first play together."

"I felt for Antiochus, poor man. He was the loser. Nobody loved him. And he loved them both."

"Racine understood loss, didn't he?"

"It seems to me he understood passion in all its diversity."

"I wonder why he had such a bad reputation. He was a mean bastard to those who befriended him."

"It may be because he was afraid he loved too much. People who behave badly often don't do it for any other reason but because they are afraid for themselves. Some people strike out before others strike out against them."

"What are you doing later?"

"I'm not sure. I still have to study for a few other exams. This was my first."

"You'll let me know."

"Of course. Meanwhile, you'll be busy grading. I don't want to distract you from that task."

"I'll be fine. Just let me hear from you."

Chapter Twenty-Three

Peter's class was busy doing their exam. Peter sat up front, his legs all over the place, busy staring at me in his usual disgruntled fashion. He had not won our last encounter and he wasn't sure what that meant for his passing the course. He was in a state. He kept hoping I would spend my time staring at his crotch. It was almost impossible not to do so. But I played the game and didn't. Which made him even more disgruntled.

After a while, he couldn't take it. He came up to me and whispered in my ear: "Hi, teach."

"Don't worry, Peter. All is well."

"Yes, but you frustrated me and I can't keep my mind on the exam."

"You'd better do so if you know what's good for you."

"What's good for me is you."

"Peter, stop now or I'll disqualify you."

"I'm going to the john and I'm going to jerk off."

"Save the energy for the exam."

"I can't concentrate. All I can think of is you."

"In French, I hope."

He walked out of the room, pouting, and I sincerely hoped he would not stay out too long. I didn't want to have to fail him. I wanted desperately to pass him and send him on his way. I was also hoping that no one would notice what had gone on between us. No worry. They were also busy with their exams.

After another twenty minutes, I walked out of class and into the john. I had to get him back. He was obviously in a booth. I stood in front of it, hoping no one would come in. "Peter, come on back. Stop making me nervous."

His door slid open and he was sitting there with an enormous erection. "Kiss it and I'll come back."

"You must be insane. You idiot! Out of here."

I left the bathroom and walked back into class, very nearly trembling with anger. He followed me and went back to the exam. His crotch was so swollen that it seemed he was getting ready to write his exam with his penis. I couldn't help smiling.

He, too, waited to give his paper in after the others had left.

"You're going to make a nervous wreck out of me, young man. You're driving me batty. How dare you behave this way."

"I can't help myself. I just can't help it. I want to have you. I don't even care about the exam any more or the grade. I just want to be with you."

"Peter, now really, you know you have other plans."

"I used to. Something's happened to me."

"You didn't drink a potion, did you? This reminds me of Tristan and Isolde."

"I drank a lot. Who knows what was in it? Maybe you're like a witch making me feel all passionate for you."

"We'll go out and find an antidote."

"The antidote is the orgasm."

"No, my dear. You don't understand the meaning of antidote."

"We'll talk about it."

"I have to go home now and have the peace of mind to mark these papers."

"When will you mark mine?"

"Some time this evening."

"Can I come over and watch you mark?"

"Absolutely not."

"Can I call you to find out the result?"

"Yes."

"When?"

"Let's say around nine o'clock."

"Okay. Then can I come over?"

"I doubt it."

"Why not?"

"I'm not marking yours last. I'm doing yours early so that you'll get off my back."

"Well then mark mine later, but let me come over."

"We'll talk about it later."

"I'll call you at nine. Please be kind."

"Just as kind as you have been."

"I wanted to be kind. I can't help how I feel. I'm a passionate fella."

"We know. But you're also a bit of a bore."

"It may give you pleasure to hurt me but I thought you were a nice man. I didn't know you had this mean streak in you."

"Mean streak!"

"Yes. You know I'm crazy about you. And you don't care."

"How do you know I don't care?"

"Well you treat me like a Neanderthal man."

"That's how you behave."

"I don't have any other experience. You're my first. And if anybody had ever told me that I could get goofy over a

French teacher, let alone a man, I would have said they lost their marbles."

"I'm very nervous about all this, Peter. I don't know where it's leading. I thought you only wanted to get a good grade and get out of here and then lead the rest of your charmed life with this president's daughter."

"That's what I thought. I don't even think about her any more. What does she mean to me?"

"You might just find that out if you spent a little more time with her."

"I don't care about that."

"Peter, be reasonable. What future would there be for you and me?"

"I could go to graduate school and I'd visit you."

"Yes, but where would we go from there?"

"Lots of men have secret relationships."

"Oh, do they?"

"Especially in the sports world. Five out of ten football players prefer guys to dolls."

"I didn't know that."

"Nobody does, but it's a fact."

"Could you live that way, Peter? Could you ruin your image? Could you taint your future?"

"I don't know. But, I'm willing to try."

"I'm not. I don't want a football player for my lover."

"Why not? We're good in bed. We have feelings, too."

"Of course you do. But society doesn't condone it."

"I thought you were above society."

"I might be but I doubt you would, in the long run."

"You just don't trust me. You think I'm a devious bastard. Maybe I was in the beginning but I've changed."

"Peter, what will happen when I pass you and you graduate?"

"I'll love you even more. I'll love you even if you fail me."

"Do you mean that?"

He sat down at my desk and placed his head in his hands. He was crying, noticeably crying. I had touched something in this creature. I decided to be nicer with him. Even if he were playing a game, he certainly was willing to carry it far. I place my hand on his shoulder. I threw caution to the wind.

"You can come over at nine. We'll spend a little time together. If you promise to go when I ask you to, I promise you I'll be very nice to you."

He got up, took me in his arms and continued sobbing. I discreetly disentangled myself.

"Get hold of yourself, sweetheart. Promise me you'll get a little rest before you come over. Can you rest?"

He nodded without speaking and left the room. I gathered up my papers and walked slowly home through the campus. I was undone.

Chapter Twenty-Four

I marked furiously so that I could compare paper to paper in the one class. I went so fast that I started Don's class as well. By nine, I had completed them all. What a relief! Now I only had one more exam to give and there were no personal favorites in that class. Peter had done rather well, somewhere in the eighties and it was with a sigh of relief that I decided to pass him once and for all. What a genuine relief.

Now I had only to meet with him and see what the passing grade would do for his morale and behavior and then find the way to keep Don from coming over early. That would be easier. The door was knocked upon and I went to answer it. It was Antonio. I nearly passed out with nervousness.

"I'm not free, Antonio. This is final examination time at the university and we're all very busy. I'm so sorry."

He looked as if he didn't believe me. He just stood there.

"Perhaps you could come over some other time."

"I need to talk to you, sir."

"Fine. If that's all it is, start talking now. I'm expecting someone in just a few moments."

"I just wanted to say that I need to be alone with you. You don't seem to want me as much as your friend does. And that makes me feel very sad."

"I'm just busier than he is, Antonio."

"I don't believe you. You think I am low class and a foreigner. And you don't want to be with me. You only do it for him."

"No, no, Antonio, but I am very shy. I am not as sure of myself as my young friend. And I know I could never twirl a pizza the way you do."

"I could teach you."

"It's not really what I want to learn."

"Do you think it is an inferior thing to do?"

"Not at all. When you do it, it becomes a genuine art."

"You are very kind. I just wish to know if you will allow me to be alone with you some time."

"Yes, yes, but not this week. I'm so overworked."

"Whenever you like. I do not wish to disturb you. I just want you to know that I want to be alone with you."

"Why, Antonio?"

"Because you make me feel very strange and very wonderful, as they say in America."

"Thank you, my friend."

"I will go now. Before I do, may I place my arms around you?"

"Antonio, you're making me nervous. I expect someone here soon."

"I will be quick. I will be very quick."

He took me in his arms and kissed my forehead, my eyelids and my neck. "You have beautiful skin, like a woman."

"Yes, I have my mother's skin. That's all I have."

"You have more. You are civilized. You are genuine person. You don't play with people's feelings."

"Thank you, Antonio. Bless you."

"If you tell me you do not want me, I will leave you alone. But I must tell you I want you."

At that moment, the door was opened by Peter. The look on his face when he saw Antonio was full of suffering.

"Well, my next appointment has arrived. Antonio, I will be in touch."

"Thank you, sir." As he left, he saluted Peter.

Peter stared at me like a jealous lover.

"Who the hell was that?"

"You're not the only student I know."

"He didn't look like a student."

"Well observed."

"Who the hell is he? If he has designs on you, I'll kill him."

"Down boy. He's a caterer. I'm giving a party graduation night and he's doing the catering."

"He doesn't look like a caterer."

"Peter, I told you that I would be nice if you behaved. If you don't, I'm afraid..."

"I'm a nervous wreck. Can't you see that?"

"Peter, my dear friend, you have passed with flying colors and I shall be happy to give you a B in the course."

Peter was dumbstruck. He sat down on the couch and started sobbing again.

"Why are you so emotional about all this?"

"I don't know. I think I'm having a nervous breakdown."

"Peter, please."

"Sit down with me and hold me in your arms."

"I thought you were a mucho macho."

"So did I. But all this has been too much for me. I just wanted to please you. I worked so hard. I can't believe I did it."

"Well, you did. You were capable of learning. You're a great guy."

He got down on his knees in front of me and went on sobbing. I lifted him up and asked him what he wanted to drink.

"Can we have some champagne?"

"If you like."

"Good."

"I have a bottle of Veuve Cliquot in there that I was saving for a special occasion. I think this is the special occasion." Suddenly I knew it was.

He opened the bottle and poured the lovely golden liquid into two champagne glasses that also were the right temperature. I insisted on a toast and we stood there drinking the elixir.

He pulled me down the corridor and threw me on the bed. Then he brought the bottle and the glasses. He started methodically taking his clothes off. In a moment, he was stark naked and sitting on the bed, sipping the champagne. I followed suit. He took the bottle and poured a good bit of it all over our bodies. Then he carefully started licking it off mine and beckoned me to do the same for him. I got up, ran out to the door and locked it carefully. When I returned, Peter was ready for serendipity.

"What do you want, Peter?"

"I want to dip my wickie."

"Then dip it. Serendip it."

We both became slightly silly and before I knew it, we were as one, joined to one another. It went very slowly and very delicately. It was miraculously smooth and somehow different from anything else I had ever known. Perhaps it was the champagne, perhaps the tears, perhaps the intensity of emotion. Peter had been transformed into a new human being, one I never thought could be there. He was himself so moved that he could not stop crying. The tears mixed with the champagne and the sperm. When the phone rang, I didn't answer it. It was probably Don's voice at the other end. I would call him later. For the moment, I felt as if I could not do anything but live the present scenario for the essential moment that it was. Peter thanked me for not answering and we held each other as if there were no tomorrow.

After a while, he got up, dressed quietly and came in to say goodnight to me. I made believe I was already asleep. He kissed me tenderly on my behind and then left. I went in for some coffee, drank it slowly and then called Don.

"Sorry, I thought it was you, but I was in the middle of it all and didn't want to lose my train of thought."

"I suspected as much, but I had promised to call. I'm still working on my other exams. See you tomorrow?"

"Certainly."

"I love you."

"I love you, too."

"A bushel and a peck?"

"How much is that?"

"You'll find out."

"Ciao, bambino."

"That's Antonio talk."

"I think I want him to cater my party."

"Then you'll have to invite him to the soirée."

"Of course. He has to see what the high life is like."

"We'll see it together."

"Good luck with your studying."

"Good luck with your marking."

"Sweet dreams."

"The sweetest."

After he hung up, I sat there, trembling slightly, wondering how far all this would go.

Chapter Twenty-Five

The dulcet tones and sprightly harmonies of Schumann's *Carnaval* reverberated through the house. Anne was practicing the magnum opus. Don and I were in attendance. I was busy explaining it all to Don, as if I were giving a class. Anne would add her two cents whenever it seemed appropriate. One day I would teach a class on literature and the music it inspired.

"*Carnaval* is the highpoint of romanticism, the ne plus ultra of romantic musical feeling. Schumann finished it at Carnival time in 1835. He was in love with the great pianist, Clara Wieck and he was also having a flirtation with a student of Wieck's father, Ernestine. When Franz Liszt heard Clara play *Carnaval*, he proclaimed it one of the greatest works he knew. It's just the sort of piece we should study in depth at the university. There are so many fascinating aspects to it. And it's perfect for graduation time. The last section called the 'March of the Davidsbündler against the Philistines' is perfect for the academic procession at graduation. It's much more effective than 'Gaudeamus Igitur'."

"I'm overwhelmed," Don proclaimed.

"You're underwhelmed. It reminds me of Tallulah Bankhead's famous dictum: There's less to this than meets the eye."

"Very funny. But that's not true."

"Every section has a content. This is typical of the intellectual romantic era. I call it high analytical romanticism. It goes extremely well with the work of George Sand, as well."

Anne was in her element. "I don't know when I've enjoyed playing this more. Finally to have it understood. Do you think everyone who comes will understand it?"

"I'm going to provide them with copious program notes. This will be the ultimate learning experience of the semester. And Elizabeth, who knows the work by heart, is choreographing it to be performed while you play."

"Won't that be distracting?" asked Don.

"Not really. It will be more fun and will help people to feel the music even more intensely."

"I like the idea," Anne chimed in. "But we're going to have to do quite a bit of rehearsing."

"We still have till the weekend. It will fall into place. I want the dancers to express things that have happened in their lives, as a kind of therapy."

"It sounds like you should have rehearsed for months," Don stated.

"Not really. Everything really valid falls into place rather quickly. The people here are rather inventive."

Anne continued to play and we were enchanted.

"Come to think of it, it does sound like ballet music. It certainly is highly impressionistic," Don said, always trying to be above it all.

"That's not the right term," Anne added, "but let's hear more about it. Proceed, maestro."

"There are all sorts of symbols and place names suggested. Ernestine was born in Asch and the four most important tones reflect just that. A flat, S=E flat, C and H=B natural. The work was dedicated to Karol Lipinski who was Paganini's only rival as violin virtuoso. 'The Préambule' (note that every section's name is in French, which is surprising coming from the German, Schumann) was inspired by the other great romantic composer, Schubert.

"Then we have section 2: Pierrot and Arlequin, two of the leading figures of the *Commedia dell'Arte*. Pierrot was the clown, a pathetic figure, always unhappy, which reminds me of one of my students, whose name is also Peter, always taking a few strides and falling over his own feet. Arlequin might as well be Andrew, the campus lover."

"It's fabulous. I wish I could have written a term paper on it."

"I'll assign it to someone one day. Then comes the Valse noble, full of spiritual longing. It continues the A, E flat, B and C. There is no romantic music without noble longing."

"Immediately afterward, we have the two sections which discuss our heroes, Eusebius and Florestan. They were the two separate contrasting natures of Schumann. Poor man died insane and was surely schizophrenic. In his youth, he noticed his two selves and exploited their romantic dichotomy. Eusebius was a dreamer, dreamily reflective and Florestan was the virtuous and vigorous man of action. I am surely Eusebius, Don and you are Florestan, and Elizabeth will choreograph us."

"I can't wait."

Anne played the two sections. She tended to play each as I talked about it. Then she would continue playing parts of each as I spoke. They were all quite short. None was longer than four minutes, most were a little more than one. Yet what treasures were infused into these small bits of time.

"'Coquette' is next. A flirtatious dancer who shows her impatience by stamping her feet vigorously. Her vacillations are played up."

"That's me," Anne proclaimed. "But I can't dance and play, as well."

"Someone will dance for you. Your fingers will be dancing, as in so much of the work." And for Don's benefit: "It's a virtuoso piece and few can play it. Gyorgy Sandor, Arturo Michelangeli. Few pianists attempt it."

"I'm going to play it in recital next year. This is my maiden voyage," Anne announced.

"Don't forget," Don quipped. "Life is too short to spend two Carnavals in Meedletown."

"Very funny. Don't kill my train of thought."

"Continue, maestro and maestra."

"Next is 'Réplique-Answer' continuing the mood of Coquette. And then 'Papillon', flirtatious as a butterfly, and then the Dancing Letters, 'Asch-Scha', which makes me think of our campus shenanigans. The most difficult thing for me is to accept the seriousness of what goes on here. It's full of *Sturm und Drang*, German romanticism at its worst, but hardly to be taken seriously."

"Unless you're personally involved," protested Don.

"Even if you are personally involved."

"You think only things that happen in the big city are worth it. You're prejudiced."

"Life is a comedy for those who think and a tragedy for those who feel."

"But all of us feel at one time or another, don't we?" Anne protested.

"There are degrees in all things, aren't there?" I added, to get back the focus on my analysis.

"We keep sidetracking you, but it gives the pianist a bit of rest."

"Now the work hots up. Chiarina is a tribute to Clara Wieck. I think of Anne."

She blushed. "I do love this section."

"And then my very favorite section, called 'Chopin'. It is more authentically Chopin than anything Chopin ever wrote. At the time Chopin was not particularly admired and German critics were brutal to him. Schumann, who had true sensibility, hailed his greatness. It is one of the most tender pieces ever written. People can hardly believe it was not written by Chopin himself."

Anne performed it with tender abandon. I kissed her cheek as she played and Don kissed the other one, to make it perfect.

"From this point on, it is pure genius. Estrella is a portrait of Ernestine, full of poetry. And then my second favorite part, the one I wanted to learn to play because it is so rhythmically fascinating. It is called Reconnaissance-gratitude and is known as a lover's meeting."

Anne played the baroque piece with the skipping obbligato and we all three sang it.

"The truth about true romantic music is that it was always singable and danceable."

"From here we go back to the *Commedia dell'Arte*. Pantalone et Colombine. This could be the caricature of the Venetian merchant the young lover of Columbine-Harlequin. I would cast Barlow and Johann. Elizabeth promised me she would see to it. They'll love being part of it all."

"It's too bad we can't film it," Don added.

"I'll try to have that done. Though the theater department and the music department might want to get in on the act."

"And serve beer and pretzels."

"We're going to have a few choices and very fancy pizzas with caviar and mushrooms."

"Now there are only a few parts left. The *valse allemande* and the Paganini intermezzo are inspired by Schumann's early work and Paganini. This was the inspiration for Schumann's musical career. He could have decided to become a critic. Fortunately for us, he didn't. The literary part of his life was valid but he was too great a composer to stop there."

"I feel as if we have entered the soul of the music."

"I hope you will."

"Listen," Anne protested. "You have plenty of time to discuss it later."

"Then l'Aveu, the confession of love. And a wonderful balletic sequence, Promenade, a stroll through a ballroom, arm-in-arm with one's partner. This, you and I shall do," I said to Don. "Elizabeth is choreographing it for us."

We went down the corridor and back, in high fettle.

"Then a short pause which leads to the grand finale: the 'March of the Davidsbündler against the Philistines'. This is the music we're going to impose on the music department for the academic procession."

"Who are the Philistines?" Don asked.

"The Davidsbündler was an association dreamed up by the critic Jean-Paul Richter. He and Schumann realized everyone had a dual nature and they took the name of the biblical king who was both deeply intellectual and a ferocious fighter. The aim of the association was to fight outmoded pedantry and the cruelty of society. In nineteenth-century Germany, a Philistine was the man who had settled down and complacently accepted the status quo. Isn't that apropos?"

"Fabulous," Don echoed.

Anne played the finale with incredible panache. Hearing her, you would have been sure the pianist was a broad-shouldered man.

"We've done it."

When she finished, the two of us applauded madly and then lifted her off the piano bench and carried her down the corridor and back. We toasted her and then all three fell in a heap on the couch, exhausted by art and erudition.

"Wait till Elizabeth finishes with us." I kissed them both.

Chapter Twenty-Six

Elizabeth was in her element. Everyone was in tights, ready to go. She had insisted on that one thing, no matter how we were shaped. After all, this was not the big time. We were interpreting the meanings of a great piece of music through significant movement.

"Now, my dears, first, thank you for coming. We will be listening to the music as played by Mlle Anne Rampart. There are more than twenty sections and we will attempt to give them meaning through movement. Remember, this is not ballet, but rather modern dance. Neither one nor the other, in reality, but something which will give us the illusion of interpreting the music."

"Bravo," came the voice of Paul Barlow. "If only we had a Diaghilev in our midst."

"The trouble with you, Paul, is that you always aim too high," came the voice of Helmut.

"*Semper gloriosus*," Paul answered. All the banter helped put everyone in a great mood.

"I have asked Anne, if we may call you by your given name," said Elizabeth, full of her customary brio, "to play the piece for us through, naming each section before she does so, in order that you may locate the section or sections you will be interpreting."

Anne went to the piano. Don held the score and called out each name clearly before it was performed. Elizabeth had given out the performers' tasks which I had xeroxed myself. This was almost as complicated as *The Cherry Orchard* and there were even some of us who had performed in both. Everyone applauded and we began. I felt the sensation of a proud parent. Don and I were Eusebius and Florestan. I was amazed at the facility with which we moved together. It was like going down the corridor over and over again and we just fell in with one another's movements. I could see that Elizabeth was delighted. She had never been able to make me do very much in her dance classes but she did imagine that she was responsible for my new found grace.

"You are definitely making progress, my dear. Your young friend is grace itself. I've never seen him before."

"I have a knack for finding talent," I said, winking to her.

She winked back, not exactly understanding what she was winking about. Don just did a few pliés. I whispered to him. "Another talent."

"My family sent us all to dance class when we were very young. My mother once wanted to be a dancer."

"It's all in the genes."

Barlow and Johann were all eyes, all ears, wondering what was coming off. They would question me later, of course. But it was the end of the season and I didn't feel so vulnerable any more.

Carolyn did a very funny coquette. She was naturally awkward, the kind of awkwardness that is close to grace. It made her, naturally funny and naturally delightful. She was never quite aware of how naturally funny she was. Her coquette was an immediate delight and everyone applauded her. Our own group was immensely grateful to her for having damaged the novelist culprit's dress with her glass of punch. She could do no wrong.

Beatrice did the Chiarina with great dignity. Her natural longing was perfectly cast with this music. Her husband hadn't yet left her and her longing for the other men metamorphosed beautifully into this short sequence. Her blond hair looked wonderful in black. When she finished her section, several of us took turns hugging her.

The Chopin sequence was given to Don alone, suddenly, and he did it up proud. I realized once again that I was linked with a young man of such grace that he could express it in painting, music, dance, jazz. The simple truth was that talent of any kind was a subtle gift which could express itself in myriad ways and forms. Eloquent writers were fine painters. Painters were masters of choice words. Talent was a rarity. Motivation and desire were, however, rarer. Don could do anything but he didn't especially care to. Motivation was more important than talent, in the long run.

The rhythmic 'Reconnaissance' was performed by several of Elizabeth's pride and joys. They were undergraduates who could skip and run and jump. Their enthusiasm was infectious and everyone started skipping to the music. If we had had time, we might have had the entire company perform in this one. I felt my pulse run fast and experienced that rare rush of joy which makes anything possible. Paul, who never skipped or jumped, allowed himself to wax enthusiastic.

"This is much better than I thought it was going to be. You are somewhat of a genius, Elizabeth."

"All depends on our raw materials, you know. As in a Chekhov play, you are as good as the weakest link in the ensemble. And here, motivation will strengthen everything. I suggest you move a bit, too, my friend. Your ultimate health will benefit immensely. You'll see."

"Checkmate," added Edward Wallace, twinkling.

He was older than Paul but lithe on his feet and I wondered what he would be doing in his sequences to come. Barlow did Pantalone as if he were a pachyderm and Wallace played another sort of pixie-like elder. An exquisite young lady played Columbine and danced in and out of their sequences.

'The Aveu', that confession of love, was thrown to Johann, who made believe he was in love with the young Columbine beauty. One noticed readily that Johann was a very handsome man. His Germanic quality did not hide that. No one could give a better imitation of a man yearning for a woman. How well he played that!

'The Promenade' went to Don and myself. We walked down the proverbial corridor again and again and again. It was slow and stately and divinely apt. We almost didn't have to be choreographed. Elizabeth invited us to improvise. All of our lovemaking had had its effect. We moved like angels together. I kept thinking how Peter would have handled it. He was a natural for the awkward Pierrot. I wondered whether he would see the show. I didn't dare to suggest to Elizabeth that he be part of it. If I were a choreographer, I would have given parts to Peter and Antonio, but in that case I would have had to be more of a dancer than I was in reality. I could only dance well if my partner led me well. I was only as good as my vis-à-vis. In a sense, I didn't exist without them. I was simply always *numero due*.

It even seemed to me that I couldn't have taught without focusing on one person in the audience, one in the class. There was no other way to do it. If the inamorata was there, all went swimmingly. If not, I was at sea. Perhaps I was unfair to myself, but I knew that I depended entirely on them. Perhaps that was why they were so good to me. They sensed my need. I was never able to do things by myself. If they knew this, they would perhaps all leave me in an instant. I never really believed that Don or Peter or Antonio or Anne ever needed me. They sensed my shyness, my refusal to impose myself. They responded to my subtlety, to my quiet need. I fit in with their needs. What would happen to me if they stopped needing me?

'The March of the Davidsbündler' was a triumph. The entire company performed in it, led by Paul Barlow and Helmut Schoen, in academic garb. We all marched triumphantly. And when it was over, everyone applauded Anne and themselves. It was already a triumph.

"We have done it," I proclaimed, joyous.

"You have done it," Elizabeth curtsied to Anne and to me. Anne took a bow, then both of us, then Elizabeth with both of us. Everyone applauded everyone else.

The weekend continued with intense individual rehearsals and then with a dreadful dress rehearsal in which everyone seemed to do the wrong thing. I reminded them all that bad dress rehearsals usually made for a triumphant performance. We were all exhausted and dispersed. Graduation was scheduled for the next morning at eleven. There were still so many things to do. Don decided to get a little shut-eye for once. The performance and party would be wildly exhausting.

I walked home in the late evening darkness, with Anne in hand. She was staying at Helmut and Elizabeth's but needed to have a walk before turning in. As we turned into my street, I caught, in sudden realization, a glimpse of Peter, hovering around my house. I immediately turned volte-face and walked her back to the Schoens. We were full of compliments for each other. She had decided to be very good. Tomorrow, her professor from Yale was coming up to hear the concert and she wished to introduce me to him.

"He may be my first husband. I have to impress him."

"You certainly will, my dear. Now get a good night's sleep."

"I don't want to. I want to talk all night long with my hosts. They're the most delightful people I've ever met. Full of Austro-Hungarian malice. How delightful."

I kissed her on the cheek and practically ran home.

Peter was there, sitting on the stairs. I stood in front of him. He smiled wanly. I did as much. We walked up to the apartment.

"I came to see you tonight because my parents will be here for graduation and so will she and her parents and I may not be able to talk to you for a while."

"I thought so."

"I was hoping I could spend a little time with you tonight because in a sense it's the last moment of the year. And who knows what will happen after that? May I introduce my parents to you?"

"Of course. I'd love to meet them."

He took me in his arms impetuously. "This is our last moment together, unless a miracle occurs."

I was well aware of that. I suddenly felt infinitely sad. I would have to prepare myself for so many goodbyes. How many relationships survived a certain moment or a certain place?

"I don't want to lose you. Promise me you won't reject me now."

"I can promise all I like. The one who is going to be doing the rejecting is you, Peter. Slowly and surely, or maybe fast and furious, but you'll see the error of your ways."

He slapped my face, almost too strongly, and I winced. Then he swept me up again in his arms and practically carried me into the bedroom. It was like a scene out of *Gone With The Wind*. It had all the remnants of passion. It was totally mutual and yet we both knew that it was just that moment, that it could never be the same again. This time it was I who did the crying. He couldn't wait to leave, after he had proven his incontestable masculinity. He had to be back in his dorm as fast as he could make it so that he wouldn't miss breakfast with the family. I suddenly wished that I had not rejected Don and Anne. Or had they rejected me?

Chapter Twenty-Seven

Graduation day! Such excitement. After a hard year and so many events, the liberation. I felt strange as I tossed and turned and tried to grab a little more sleep before facing the day. Don would be having breakfast with his family. Peter would be having it with his nearest and dearest as well as his girlfriends. Anne would have it with Helmut and Elizabeth and I would join them early on. That left Antonio. He was to arrive with the glorious pizzas, to be refrigerated until party time. The actual event was to take place at the elegant and beautiful Davidson Art Center. Sam Ericson had been generous with his space. We had rehearsed there, as well. The party would begin at the Arts Center and then the die-hard loyals would come over to my place.

I heard footsteps on the stairs and realized it must be Antonio. How did he manage to be ready at eight in the morning? He probably had been at work for literally hours. The door was unlocked and in he came.

"Sir?"

"Antonio, is that you?"

"Yes, sir. Not too early, I hope. I know you have a busy day."

"Thank you so much. Just put everything down and we'll arrange it together."

"I have to make several trips."

"Shall I help you?"

He peeked into the bedroom and, seeing that I was under the covers, he discreetly said no. "I will be finished bringing them all up in a few minutes."

"I'll take a shower and be ready to help you."

"Just stay there, please. Don't move."

I could hear all the things being brought up. I waited patiently, thinking long and hard about this day and its significance. How nice that it would begin and perhaps even end with him. That would be a true consolation for all the abandonments. I was still feeling the sadness of Peter's departure. Don and Anne were on backburners. Would I pass muster with Don's parents? Would Anne's professor approve of me?

Antonio appeared and sat down on the edge of the bed. "How nice you look in the morning, still a little sleepy."

"How nice you look in the morning, working as hard as you do."

"I want to hold you in my arms and dream beautiful dreams."

"Go right ahead. Be my guest."

He slowly removed his clothing, folding it neatly in a pile at the edge of the bed and then slipped quietly in beside me. He held me in his arms and looked beatifically at me.

"You are a very nice man."

"You are a remarkably sweet fellow."

I felt his masculinity growing next to me and then he slowly placed it below my balls and between my legs. In a moment, he was on top of me in the missionary position. I might as well have been a woman. He treated me exactly as if I were just that, slowly moving his member between my legs, ever so sensitively. He placed his delicate lips on mine and we moved in a slowly rocking rhythm. We didn't need lubrication. He didn't feel the friction. He shut his eyes and had the quietest, sweetest orgasm. I followed suit and we lay there for the longest time. Never had I felt so much like a woman. With the others, I was always a man, even with burly Peter, for whom I was another fella. I held Antonio in my arms as if he were my child. He reverted from masculine lover to dependent child in the twinkling of a second.

I realized that time was fleeting and I would need a moment with Anne. The phone rang and it was indeed she.

"Rise and shine, sweetheart. Come over and have some of the best coffee I've ever had."

I heard Elizabeth's indulgent voice proclaiming that she was exaggerating. I promised to be over before too long. Antonio and I took a shower together, soaping each other up generously and dressing one another as we took turns being each other's valets. That was also something I had never done before. Life was full of surprises.

Then I inspected the pizzas – heavenly – and we placed them gingerly in the fridge. We drank marvelous coffee which he had the generosity to bring.

"I want you to be here for the party and help serve your creations. I want you admired."

"If you like."

"And you might want to come to the musical event."

"I thank you but I am in service today and I must do that. I will be here when you need me."

We parted in total amity. I thanked him, he thanked me and we went on to the rest of our lives. I walked calmly over to Helmut and Elizabeth's. They were laughing and carrying on.

"Welcome, dear boy. You have given us such genuine pleasure by allowing us to meet your dear Anne. She is the loveliest young lady we have met in so long, and such an artist. You must promise to have her up here as often as possible. We approve."

We toasted the day with yet another superb coffee.

"I have to get on to the graduation and first get my cap and gown," I announced.

"You should have brought it here and we would have dressed one another," Helmut proclaimed. "No one does this sort of thing better than Elizabeth."

We parted company and I walked over to my office. Anne would be in the grandstand with Elizabeth, special consideration for her imminent concert. Her professor would arrive some time in the afternoon and was instructed to go right to Helmut and Elizabeth's.

"What does he do, dear?"

"He professes the Russian language and its literature."

"How very nice. We hope he will enjoy our entertainment."

"He better," she stated with her usual verve.

I kissed and hugged them all and then went on to my office in the basement of Boylan Hall. I was beginning to feel a little nervousness, a certain stage fright which the French call *trac*.

I got out my regalia and started to put it on. Fortunately, it was a beautiful day and we could have the graduation *en plein air*. I heard footsteps again and wondered who could be down here at this hour. To my shock and surprise, it was Peter.

"Hi, teach."

"How come you're down here, Peter. I thought you were stuck with your families."

"We had an early breakfast and I thought I'd find you down here. I tried your place first. I just wanted to thank you for everything, bless you a little and tell you I'll never forget you." He gave me a huge hug.

"I'm glad you came. I was beginning to miss you."

"Me, too. You want to have a quickie?"

"Certainly not. Purity is essential on this one day of the year."

"I need it."

"Possess your soul in patience."

"I can't. I'm yearning for you."

He took out his whopper and knelt in front of me.

"Peter, what if it gets on our clothes."

"Don't worry. I'm almost ready. Just pat my head a little and tell me I'm a good boy."

I did just that and he ejaculated on to the floor.

"You're not hard to please."

"I was so nervous, I had to come. Don't you need to?"

"No. I'm older than you are."

"I'll never get that old. I'll have to come every day of my life."

"It's going to be time-consuming, Peter."

"I know, but you know me. Mr. Nervous. Mr. Sentimental."

"You're not alone."

"I've got to find you again. I'll be away for a few weeks at home and then I want to make a date with you."

"I may be in Europe."

"I'll join you."

"Where would you like to go?"

"I think I'd like Rome. It would be nice to be in your jungle, as you called it."

"We'll talk about it. It might be nice to spend a week or two in the jungle."

"It's a date."

"Cross your heart and hope to die?"

"Pie in the sky."

"I'll be in touch and we'll make the grand plan. I'm so happy. I thought you'd say no."

"I thought you didn't want to."

"Of course I want to. We have to see what our future will be, however slight."

"We have to promise to meet at least once a year."

"On Groundhog Day?"

"Why that?"

"I don't know."

"We'll take annual vacations together. I'll tell Susie I had to be free to have dates with the boys."

"I see you've got this all organized."

"Not really. But if I don't get free time with you, I won't be able to make commitments elsewhere."

"Now help me on with my uniform."

Peter did and he was rather good at it. "You look nifty."

We left separately and vowed eternal loyalty.

I went up to the gathering place of the faculty. It was wonderful walking on campus in full regalia. Paul Barlow fell in step with me and we listened to the strains of the marching music.

"Your ballet was quite smart."

"Thank you. We worked so hard."

"I think your new relationship is quite smart, too."

"Don't dramatize. It may be quite smart but it's also quite of the moment."

"Better this than solitude."

He seemed suddenly terribly melancholy. I had to say something meaningful. "You're the most brilliant of us all, Paul. The rest of us are just amateurs, as you always tell us."

"Yes, but you're having more fun in life than I am."

"We may be seeming to, but only literature counts. *Ars longa, vita brevis.*"

"*Vita longa, ars brevis.*"

"You're coining a phrase."

"I'm very depressed."

"Whatever for?"

"Aram is leaving Beatrice. That terrible novelist has done her dirty work."

"He would have done it any way. Maybe now she'll have a better life."

"I doubt it. People are so destructive."

"Don't worry. She'll have more time for you."

"Bitch."

"I mean it. You need your friends full time."

We arrived at the robing room and it was moments before we were ready for the academic procession.

Schumann's 'Davidsbündler' finale was the rousing music. It made me joyous. I kept wanting to scream out: "My God, we've done it." As we walked out and down to our places, I saw so many familiar faces. Carolyn winked at me. Elizabeth and Anne were like two distinguished ladies of the court. I thought I saw Don, surrounded by two people, mother and father who were characters right out of Normal, Norman Rockwell. Perhaps I was mistaken.

We were treated to the usual homilies and speeches. President Butterworth was particularly eloquent about the approaching 1960s, what we hoped would be a better time for our country and our university. I escaped into my own thoughts. I felt all warm inside, as if I had lived through an eon of events. I could only imagine what our evening would be like. As we marched out and were on our way to the reception for the graduates and the honored guests, I came upon Peter and his family. What a handsome group of people. A father with a mane of gray hair and a mother who had been a great beauty. He winked at me. I tried to sight Don and family but I knew that I would surely find them at the reception. I had to have strength and fortitude. The next hours would be crucial.

Chapter Twenty-Eight

Elizabeth, Anne and I stuck close to the punch bowl and the hors d'oeuvre table. For some reason, I was ferociously hungry. They had tiny sausages and some lovely deviled eggs. I knew why suddenly. I had never had time for breakfast. Not even a crust of pizza. Sex and stress made one especially hungry.

Each of the teachers greeted their students and families as well as friends. I waited patiently for mine to find me. Beatrice and Paul meandered by. She looked as if she had been crying all night. I kissed her fervently. She smiled wanly. Paul was properly solemn. Johann arrived with his friend. They were cordial, as ever. Harry avoided me, still blaming me for Dana's departure. Sam and Beulah were delightful. They were ready for our arrival at the art center. Sig Nachman was perfunctorily friendly. He had probably investigated the cause of the stir the night of the distinguished professor's speech and saw me as a culprit. Helmut took up his rightful position on the other side of Elizabeth. I wished each group could have been officially painted for the moment.

Peter finally appeared with his dashing parents, his girl Susie and the president of the college and his wife. I and my group were introduced around. Peter's gracious father took a moment to thank me for his son's graduation.

"I've been wanting to meet the gentleman who made it possible for Peter to get through the French language. I can tell you we were worried. You must be quite a teacher."

Susie put in her word: "I kept telling him an educated man must be conversant with French, *n'est-ce pas*? He promised me."

Peter and I refrained from comment. We smiled around and at each other. I finally felt compelled to say something.

"French is like bicycle riding. If you ever knew any, you don't forget it. You just start flexing your muscles again. Peter didn't learn it all in a few weeks. It was lurking there."

Nobody believed me but they looked with pride at their magnificent specimen of a son. We had nothing much more to say. I wished them all well.

Anne looked after them and so did Elizabeth. "That guy is some hunk. He even looks sensitive," Anne ventured.

"He might have had quite a moment in the 'Aveu'. Lovesick people look better if they have a little flesh on them," Elizabeth pontificated. "Why didn't you suggest him?"

"I don't like my students competing with each other. I don't think Don would have enjoyed competition."

Anne looked at me intently. "I should think not. That is if he were competition." I winked at her.

"Where is Don?" asked Elizabeth. "I haven't had a glimpse of him all morning."

"Neither have I," I added suddenly worried that he might have defected in some way. But then he appeared with his parents, the very Norman Rockwell group I thought I'd glimpsed. He made his way to us and presented us all around. His parents looked at me with curiosity in their eyes. I thought I even saw a little hostility. They were beady-eyed and conventionally good looking. I saw how much Don respected them and I wondered what it boded for our relationship. I didn't even dare to look directly at him. I allowed Anne to lean over and kiss him, which she did in front of the parents.

"So it's you," said the mother, as if she had just caught sight of a mortal enemy. "We've heard a great deal about you, young lady. I wish Don had brought you home to us so that we might have gotten acquainted."

"He never asked," she said candidly.

"I guess he wasn't sure what kind of welcome you would have gotten. Did he meet your parents, my dear?"

"No. Not really."

Elizabeth felt needed. She came through. "Meeting families is one of the most difficult things in life. It should be avoided unless absolutely necessary."

"Elizabeth," Helmut protested and offered punch to the entire gathering. I knew I would have to say something to the parents eventually but I hoped I would not have to.

"And you're the Bohemian French professor. My my, we're getting to meet everybody you forget to introduce us to, Don."

"Bohemian?" I echoed. "No no. Hungarian."

"Isn't that the same thing?" Elizabeth quipped.

"Your son has a few bohemian sides to him, too," I added.

Don blushed crimson. Fortunately, his parents didn't seem to notice.

It was the father's turn. "We're very happy that Don has had such a fine education and met such fine people. He'll have happy memories of his school years. He writes us the nicest letters about you all."

The mother's lips turned quince. "He might as well know a little about life before he settles down to be a productive member of society."

I wanted to kick her but that would have endangered something between Don and me. I finally understand the sources of his rebellion. How could he not see how valid they were? My heart sank more and more.

Don did not seem to be willing to enter into the conversation. Would I have to console him? He seemed to wish to show his parents that he had known Anne very well. He took her arm and marched her over to another table. I found that unbearable and I slunk into a kind of blue apathy. Had it not been for Elizabeth and Helmut, I might simply have walked off into the afternoon sunlight.

"Are there no artists in your family?" asked Helmut.

"Not that I recall" said his mother.

"Aunt Hortense certainly had a talent for watercolors," added the father, warming my heart.

"We all have a talent for something," his wife added, "but we don't exaggerate."

"What a pity!" Elizabeth countered. "Exaggeration is a necessary part of life, especially when one is growing up."

"Moral rectitude precludes exaggeration."

"Without exaggeration, one cannot understand moral rectitude," I added, realizing the jig was up.

But Don's mother was willing to argue it out. "My son was always an exaggerator. We were always worried about him. He needed moral counseling from an early age and that is what worries us about him. He has a few loose screws, as you might say, and I am really grateful to you all for protecting him as you do. He's really a very good boy, but he has a wild side to his nature."

I finally understood. "Don't worry about him. Basically, deep down, he's full of guilt."

"How would you know," the mother continued.

"Oh, give us a little credit for elementary psychology."

"But you're a French professor, not a psychology professor."

"I can see you've not read French novels," Elizabeth helped.

"I haven't had the time or the inclination."

"Perhaps you will some day. That would have helped you to be a functioning mother," Elizabeth added.

War had been declared. I waved to Anne and Don and they came to our rescue.

"We must get ready for our performance," Elizabeth said, playing director. "Will you two be coming to it?"

"It's just a little late for us. We promised to visit one of our cousins in nearby Hartford."

"Oh, what a pity," Elizabeth chirped.

"We need our audience," Anne added. "We worked so hard for all this."

"What you need is a bohemian audience and you probably have that right here at the university."

Off they went and off we went and I held Anne's arm tightly.

"Aren't you glad you never had them for in-laws?" I asked.

"*Quelle horreur*! as they say at home."

"And he's such a charming young man," Elizabeth added.

I asked Anne: "What were you two talking about?"

"I think Don was in a fright. He was afraid his parents had insulted me and he thought you were on his mother's list as well. I tried to reassure him. I don't think I did a very good job. But now I think I understand a lot of things. Why he left me after latching on to me. Why he latched on to you."

"And why he'll leave me... She's formidable."

"Don't blame it on her. Your little friend, Don, has probably scared them out of their wits when he was a tiny tot," said Anne, suddenly realizing the truth.

"Heredity or environment, the great question," Elizabeth stated.

"It's a little bit of both. But it has a lot to do with an individual, as well," I added.

"I think we're all born into the wrong families. It's a test of character."

"How unusual to be discussing all this at a graduation," Helmut added, whimsical.

"What better time?" Elizabeth looked up at him. "It's the day of reckoning, after all."

Don ran up and squeezed my arm, pushing his way between Anne and me. "I'm sorry. I think my Mother should be taken in small doses."

"Like castor oil," I added.

"Did she do it to you, too?" he asked.

"I know you tried to deflect the center of interest to Anne, but I think you may have talked about me to her on more than one occasion."

"I'm so proud of you," he pleaded.

"Well, that explains it. Are there any ministers in your family?"

"One or two."

"On your mother's side?"

"Yes."

"Well, she speaks about you as if you were once an axe murderer."

"What did she tell you?"

"Nothing. She just hinted you had had a past."

"Let us not deflect interest from our performance. We may handle the vagaries of the past when we have time for that."

We obeyed Elizabeth and went into rehearsal with a vengeance. After all, it was just a run through and we needed to get away from the unpleasantness we had just lived through.

As Anne sat down at the piano, Don whispered in my ear. "Not to worry. I love you. More than ever."

"You should have warned me," I said. "I left my armor home."

Chapter Twenty-Nine

Pink rococo. The Davidson Art Center was a perfect backdrop for *Carnaval*. Anne prevailed. She played magisterially. In the front row, facing her, was her professor. I couldn't believe this was what she would choose for herself. He was tiny, beady-eyed, ironic looking, as if the world hinged on his opinions. He half smiled but never really smiled. I knew that we should not be looking at our audience but I was well aware of every element in it. I was happy that Don's family were not part of it. They might have dragged it down. The music was deliciously romantic but it would probably not appeal to everyone. The music department came out in full force and that made me happy because they would be supportive to Don.

We did the Eusebius and Florestan sections with our customary panache. What I loved mostly for us was the Promenade. We strolled through the room with our customary cool. The audience applauded after most of the sections and was more than just polite. The curtain calls were quite brilliant. Several people stood and it easily led to a standing ovation. I felt proud, got over my fears and knew that I would soon have to take over. At any rate, I was not alone. I might be alone tomorrow but for the moment the emphasis was on the beautiful work we had done. Don and I did not look at each other but we were as one for this moment.

Everyone was kissing everyone else. Carolyn's husband, Bill, told us we ought to go on tour. The distinguished professor and his wife were among the well-wishers and all the more so because it was rumored that they were to be leaving in a month to take up residence elsewhere. They left the reception early. I could see them going out to their car as if a chapter had ended in their and our lives.

Anne's professor shook all of our hands with a strong shake. He was pleased with what he had seen. His girl was a talented lady. The reception went swimmingly. It lasted quite a time and when it showed signs of waning, I told my people to invite the die-hards back to my place. I extricated myself and went walking down there. Don promised to join me with Anne and her friend. Elizabeth and Helmut promised to arrive post-haste.

The campus by moonlight had a magic of its own. I would never forget its evocative quality. So much had happened in these hallowed halls and on these much trod walkways. There was a festive air. Parties were being held in nearly every fraternity and house. Tomorrow the campus would be somewhat abandoned. Summer would begin and with it new scripts and new ideas. I had made it a rule never to teach in summer and so to keep a freshness going. This summer I might have enjoyed it if only Don or Peter would stay. Antonio would miss Don and myself. So much was still to be resolved.

I arrived at the house, scampered up the stairs and found Antonio warming the pizzas in his quiet, thoughtful manner.

"Antonio, how nice, you're here."

"I hope your evening went as planned."

"Oh yes, it was fine."

"I hope you are now hungry."

"We may not be as hungry as I thought but I know I am."

"I brought something specially for you."

He took out an individual thin crusted pizza with scented truffles on it. "I made this for you."

We drank a glass of champagne and shared the creation. I bit into it and then gave him part of it to bite into, as well.

"I am the hired help."

"You are the creator."

"I did this for you."

"I cannot tell you how happy I am that you are here. This is splendid."

"How kind of you. My feelings are the same."

"You will be meeting many people this evening. Do not let them intimidate you."

"If you will explain what that means, I will certainly try to obey you."

"Do not let them make you feel less than what you are."

"No chance for that. When you are here, I cannot feel badly."

"Good."

"What are you doing at the end of the evening?"

"I'm not sure but I may have to be with our mutual friend, Don."

"Perhaps we can be the three of us."

"Perhaps. But I may not see him for some time. If he wishes to be alone, then I will certainly see you at another moment. I will tell you as soon as I know."

The gathering soon escalated. Anne and her professor and Don were the first to arrive and they were accompanied by Carolyn, Bill and Helmut and Elizabeth. Champagne, vodka and various beers flowed. Compliments flowed with them.

Don took me aside and told me to give him an hour alone after the party. I asked about Antonio and he gave me one of his difficult looks. "I want to be alone with you. In the morning, I'll have to see my parents and we'll be going off to Hartford and St. Louis for a while. I need a little special time with you."

Anne asked me how I liked her professor. I tried to be positive about it and him. "He thought you were wonderful. He's so pleased with my friends. I'd like you, Elizabeth and Helmut to spend some time with us in New Haven. You must promise to be with me in this episode of my life."

"Will it only be an episode?" I asked.

"Who can tell? It may be much more. I know he's difficult but he wants me and so few of them really do. Being together is different from just having a roll in the proverbial hay."

"I understand that only too well."

She was probably going to do the only possible thing. All of my lovers would get married and I would go on to new generations of disciples. I had to talk about that with Rosie and Roger.

I had met Rosie at Yaddo the summer before and she had been interested in my posing for her. Her husband Roger was a well respected critic and a very charming fellow. They sometimes shared their friends and they had invited me to their place in Woodstock. I would try to lure Don there so that we could mastermind the summer. Paris, Rome, it all beckoned. I had to believe it was all possible. Mariana Herzlich had been absolutely accurate. I would have to liberate myself from this golden campus. It had given me more than I had bargained for. But I could not go on with it bereft of the golden boys it had given me. I had invited Rosie and Roger to come this evening and they had promised to come but somehow they had not arrived. If they had, I might have had my own family there. I could have invited my parents but they were in their own way even less accommodating than Don's parents and they would have smelled a rat.

Sam and Beulah decided to join us. We all treated them as if they were royalty. Suddenly, without warning, a form of serendipity, Rosie and Roger arrived, huffing and puffing, apologizing profusely. They had missed a road or two and had not been able to get there on time. So they had come to my place. It was perfect. I sat them down with Beulah and Sam and we were soon on to the subject of painting. I could perhaps arrange for a show for Rosie. Her portraits were so remarkable. This could be a splendid place for her to have a show. The academic world was no more nor less a marketplace than anywhere else.

Sam looked over at Antonio and proclaimed him a living Caravaggio. "I didn't know there were any in Middletown."

"He creates pizzas nearby. I thought he looked like the David."

Sam gave me a quizzical look. "One couldn't know that unless one had a bird's-eye view."

I realized what I had said and we both blushed.

"You have very good taste in men," he proclaimed.

"And in women," Elizabeth added, as she passed us. There was no great love lost between them, I could see. She was doing everything to protect my name. All we have in life are allies or opposition. I was still too innocent to comprehend that.

Sam asked Anne to play the *Carnaval* again, for our intimate gathering. She was too tired but she did agree to play the Chopin section. We listened to it with adoration and then asked for the Reconnaissance. There a group of us hopped and skipped and the party went on to become even wilder. I went out to the kitchen to inform Antonio that I was unable to see him later and regretted it. He decided not to stay another minute and I accompanied him to his car. There I paid him for his endeavors and sat with him for a moment in the front seat.

"You have many fine friends."

"It is quite a place to be."

"When will I see you again?"

"I'll be by tomorrow evening, if you would like. When do you get off work?"

"Sometime after nine. Is that too late?"

"No, that's perfect. I'm going to take you for a nice meal somewhere."

"That would be amusing."

"It would be my particular pleasure."

He leaned over and fell into my arms. "Why would you be so kind to someone like me?"

"I might ask the same question."

"You are someone I could never hope to meet on a personal basis."

"I can return the compliment."

"When I am older and have a life of my own, I will always look back to this moment."

"Why aren't you married?"

"Because I don't want to be."

"But you will, eventually?"

"I will have to, for my family's sake."

"Do we live for ourselves or our families?"

"That is a great question."

"To be or not to be," I said, a little high and more than a little banal.

"That is the answer," said he.

"It is also the question."

"It is both, perhaps."

"Yes, my dear David."

"I am Antonio."

"You are even Caravaggio."

"I think you need a night's rest."

I kissed him goodnight, a kiss so passionate that he resisted it. Kissing was something both men and women did.

"You do not mean what you just did."

"Of course I do."

"Then you will have to marry me."

"I don't want to be a woman."

"Many men are doing it, I am told."

"I would only want to be a man with you, Antonio. That could cause problems for you."

"For us both."

"We will have to think about that."

"I think we already have."

I saw a silhouette near the car. It was Don. I had not done anything terrible and so I played very high.

"Take your friend to bed, Don. He is a little drunk."

Don helped me up the stairs as I played more inebriated than I was. "I came after you because I was afraid you might have gone with him."

"Where would I go? I told him he had to leave. For your sake, I did that and I had to pay him as well as thank him for what he had done. Don't you think he did a splendid job?"

"I wasn't hungry, for once. I'm too upset. We have to get in and make it look like we're the hosts."

And we did. Our arrival was the cue for most everyone to leave. Everyone lingered to praise Anne, Elizabeth and myself and Don. Each farewell became an official one and I was afraid they would still be there hours later. My energy was ebbing. Everyone proposed yet another farewell and repast. It could be a long party lasting most of the summer.

Anne and her powerful professor left next. She embraced me and made me promise I would come to New Haven when she summoned me. I said yes, of course. Helmut and Elizabeth were in their element. They had become campus stars and were at the height of their popularity on a campus where they were generally distrusted and disliked because they were crafty and European.

Beatrice and Paul, Sam and Beulah, went next. We all promised to have a fine moment together before we dispersed for the summer. Rosie and Roger were ordered to return as soon as possible for a state visit. Roger lamented that he had not been able to speak with the Caravaggio. Rosie was happy she had met Beulah and Sam. She made me promise to come soon and to bring friends with me. Then I could recount to her what all this was all about.

"You're certainly leading a complicated life, my friend. I thought Yaddo was complicated. Compared to that, this place is fraught."

"As I tried to tell you last summer. But it's gotten even worse now," I added.

"How can you bear the academic world?"

"It's the only world we writers have if we're not independently wealthy," Roger added, lucid as always. "And besides which, there is the great consolation: the students."

Bill looked at him, every bit as lucid. "That is if you don't have to mollycoddle them. Or teach them about sex, which someone always needs."

"Hallelujah," Carolyn added as an obbligato, obviously as drunk as we were.

Before too long, Don and I were alone. We breathed a sigh of relief and lay down on the rug. Don played the Brando record and we breathed heavily.

"I wish this would never end," I said.

"It's been recorded for all time."

"What do you mean?"

"I'll always remember it. The *Carnaval* party."

"What time is it?"

"It's after 2 a.m."

"The witching hour."

"The twitching hour."

We both laughed lightly. If only this night would never end. But end it would have to. And we would soon be in another life. Don rolled over to me and kissed me lightly on the cheek.

"Should I go?"

"Whatever for?"

"I don't want to overstay my welcome."

"I have hardly seen you in the last days."

"You're lucky. I've been a mess."

"Is it because of your parents?"

"Yes. My double lives coinciding."

"I understand."

"No you don't but you're nice to try."

"I'm here for you whenever you need me."

"I need you now."

"I want you to promise me you'll liberate yourself and spend some time with me this summer."

"Where?"

"We're invited to Woodstock to visit with Rosie and her husband. She's a painter. You'll have a lot in common with her."

"What about her husband?"

"He's a writer and he seems very decent."

"How long will we stay with them?"

"A few days. And then we have to spend a week or so in Paris."

"I can't afford that."

"I'm taking care of that."

"That wouldn't be fair."

"I owe you that and you owe me the time."

"You have it all figured out."

"Only if you agree."

"Be patient with me."

"I have the patience of Job."

Don shivered a little. "Job went through too much."

"Don't you think I'm going through quite a bit now?"

"And what about me?"

"Both of us."

"Let's just think about now. Let me take you down the corridor for a delicious moment together."

"A last memory?"

"A last memory... of the season."

We rose solemnly. We walked down the corridor as if it were a scene from Promenade. Then we fell on the bed and fell asleep fully clothed. When the dawn came up, Don slowly rose. He took off all his clothes, went into the shower and refreshed himself. I made believe I was sleeping. He threw me a silent kiss and left. I turned over and slept a few more hours. When I got up to the new day,

I felt like ashes and dust. It took me several hours to clean up, totally alone. I knew no one would be running up the stairs. I was bereft. I was too sad to cry.

Chapter Thirty

Rosie was mixing her paints on her home-made palette. I was posing for her, as I did at Yaddo. She enjoyed finding a likeness while skewering her poseur verbally.

"Tell me more. I love your stories. Has it been a good year at school?"

"I don't yet have a true perspective but it's been wild."

"A true perspective doesn't exist. It has to be your own perspective."

"Not only mine but all the others I encountered."

"But it has to be told through your own or it doesn't exist."

"Can't one tell it in several perspectives at once?"

"That's impossible."

"That's what Picasso tried to do, to show each element in several perspectives. That's why it all seems to be askew."

"That's fanciful, my dear. Might as well define cubism thus."

"And why not?"

"You're free to think as you wish, but let's not be childish. At any rate, tell it all from your perspective and I will try to understand."

"I'm not sure you will try. But you may be entertained."

"That's all I ask, and that's all your reader will ask."

"Isn't that a moral perspective?"

"Perhaps. Moral is a very complicated word."

"Isn't all literature moral?"

"I should hope not."

"I had a room-mate at college who maintained it was. And he was very brilliant."

"Well then, be moral. Be immoral. But tell a good story."

"The important thing is to tell the truth."

"Truth is relative."

"It was Picasso, himself, and Cocteau, as well, who maintained that art was a lie which told the truth."

"The lies of art are most beautiful."

"All this is highly theoretical. I'll go on to the story itself."

"Bravo."

"But I'm very anxious and worried because there is no outcome yet. No dénouement."

"*Ne fret pas*, as we would say in pidgin French."

"I like that."

"Well, we've gotten nowhere so far. If I were to paint you in this way, the result would be nil. But it gives me an idea. I will do several likenesses of you in the same painting. You have several looks, depending on your mood, and I shall try to capture the double or the triple you."

"My turn to say bravo. I can't wait."

"I have met several people at the same time. Each has helped me to get a perspective on the other one. I doubt I would have had one without the others."

"A fertile period, I see."

"Yes, but it is confusing. Multiplicity is always confusing."

"Start somewhere."

"*In medias res*. Classroom. I was busy trying to illuminate Racine's *Bérénice*, the most lucid tale of passion in the seventeenth century."

"Oh, those French."

"Every time I looked at a certain fellow in class, he seemed to be intent on trying to understand me personally. I soon met him in several places on campus. He played saxophone, he painted, he understood all kinds of music."

"A Renaissance man."

"He soon took to visiting me and then he introduced me to his girlfriend, a lovely creature. They spent weekends in my apartment until she became pregnant. Then he became very confused. She went home to her parents and had an abortion. But before that, we had both slept with her because she took a shine to me."

"That's not a story, it's a *roman-fleuve*. How did you condense it so quickly? Masterful."

"It baffled me because it seemed to me that they both wanted me."

"Now that's even more complicated."

"That is what happened. He seduced me and she wanted me for a friend. She is now a dear friend. And he and I have been having a mad affair which is now on the wane through no fault of anyone's. He is a mother's boy who is simply destroyed by his mother's hold on him."

"How did he ever get interested in her?"

"I'm not sure. I think he gets interested in virtually everyone for a moment. He and I would go off to have pizzas at a nearby pizza establishment and the pizza man, the one who created them, for they are genuine creations, genuine paintings of cheese and dough, came on to both of us. And we shared him, as well."

"This is positively Roman."

"Neapolitan. The pizza fellow is an immigrant who is really heterosexual but is fascinated by other forms of self-expression. He is a genuine gentleman and very sweet-natured."

"Did you make it a foursome?"

"No. She is from New York and though she has been with us for the last week – she's the pianist who played *Carnaval* – she is only aware of the first part of the equation. We all performed in the ballet of *Carnaval*, but not Antonio, the pizza maker, but he provided all the refreshments at the party you attended."

"*Dio mio!*"

"Well, there's some of it."

"There's more?"

"Yes, Don and Anne, Don and Anne and myself, Don and Antonio and myself, Don and Antonio, Antonio and myself and..."

"You may need more than one tableau."

"No. It's all part of the same picture. I just haven't decoded it yet."

"Do continue."

"I have another student named Peter. He wasn't sure to be able to pass his course. If he didn't pass, he wouldn't graduate. He expects to marry the daughter of a small college president. He decided to try to bribe me to be able to pass. He is a charming young man and that's what he basically is. But in the process of trying to bribe me, he decided that the best way was to seduce me."

"I hardly blame him."

"You mustn't take sides."

"It's no fun if you don't take sides."

"It's too early to take sides."

"That may be. Continue."

"Well, he seems to be taken by me completely. You might say he fell in love in the process. He took every opportunity to be by my side and kept seducing me in the strangest places and moments, even on graduation day."

"I never saw you as a campus Lothario. You were so sweet and almost passive at Yaddo."

"I am."

"You can't convince me of that."

"There are moments when we blossom. I'm a late bloomer."

"Very well. No judgment on that. But how did things not complicate further? Doesn't Don know about Peter and vice versa?"

"Not at all. I don't think it would have bothered Don, the more the merrier with him. But Peter would have been shattered."

"That's always a problem. The sensitivities of our proclivities."

"Exclusivity is the question. Some want to share and others will absolutely never do that."

"There are potential problems with it. I think that if you're going to have an affair, you might as well do it on your own. Learn about it and do not reveal it because it might hurt your vis-à-vis, that is if you have one."

"You were in love at Yaddo. I was the go-between."

"Yes. I was madly in love with a rotter. How could I have been so foolish?"

"You didn't have the proper perspective."

"Aren't you clever? You dear boy. You were protecting me."

"I loved you as one loves a surrogate mother. You were my artist."

"I still am, I hope. You're my muse."

"But you're a lucky woman. You're happily married and a mother."

"Never imagine you understand things from the outside. Of course, I'm happily married. But... well, anyway, it's none of your business. Tell me more about you."

"It's the end of the season. They've all gone off to their families. The two of them have graduated. I don't know how I'll see them again. Anne has met a formidable professor and she will probably marry him. Don is trying to decide whether I will be part of his future. Peter wants to spend a week with me in Rome if he can get away. He'd like an annual reunion. It boggles the mind. And Antonio would love to marry me if I got a sex change, which I would never do, not in the wildest depths of despair."

"I'm glad you came to us, my dear. You are in need of some coddling. Roger and I will do our best. And you can have any of them visit here if you see fit. If it would help you."

"I'm deeply grateful. I don't know what I would have done now that I am so alone."

"It doesn't seem as if solitude is your strong suit."

"It never has been but it is now."

"I'm enjoying this painting. It's going to be a humdinger."

"If you were me, what would you do?"

"I thought you'd never ask."

"Think about it and let me know."

"I'd marry this Anne. She might tire of her professor and she seems to be most fond of you. Then you could share life together. It isn't good to make homosexual liaisons. They rarely last and they cause so much pain. It's nice to have children and fidelity is only important if you love one another deeply. There are so many kinds of fidelity, after all."

"You've lived a lot."

"I've had to."

Roger peeked into the studio. He was a jovial fellow, full of fun and oh so literary, a specialist in so many areas of French literature, but in modern arts and letters, not in my old classical century.

"I hope I'm not disturbing. You've had a phone call."

"From someone named Don?"

"Yes. He's at your school and he wanted to know how to drive up here. I gave him instructions and he should be here in a while."

"We've got to be very nice to these boys, weirdie," she called to her husband.

"But, of course. I'll show you where the two of you can stay for as long as you like."

Rosie put down her brushes and smiled benevolently. "Enough posing for today. I think we accomplished a great deal. I'm very pleased. I think I'll go in and prepare lunch while you show Don around."

Roger took me to a nearby cabin, rustic as hell, a dream place for two people who wanted to share aloneness together.

"I understand you're having a heavy time of it all."

"Yes. I'm very confused at this point. I love this young guy and he loves me but he's not sure what that means. He's having a serious identity problem."

"That goes on all one's life, my boy."

"Must it?"

"No, but we're all more complicated than we think."

"Is it possible to love more than one person at a time?"

"Yes, of course. It's just silly to love just one. You never know what might happen. But it's fine if that's what you want. Still, temptation is everywhere and beauty is everywhere. Is this the fellow who made the pizzas? The Caravaggio?"

"No. But I have a problem there, too. He'd like to have me, as well, but he doesn't understand what it is to possess a man."

"Does anyone?"

We both laughed. "Youth is such a perplexing time. We all think it's forever."

"But when does youth end? I used to be very old when I was young. Now that I'm a bit older I feel younger than ever."

"Old age is wasted on the young. That's a conundrum, rather Shavian, I would say."

"It's Don who's arriving, the fellow who worked with me on *Carnaval*. He's a painter and a musician, as well. He's multi-talented."

"He'll have to choose something somewhere along the line."

"He doesn't know whether he wants to be an artist. I think he might be happier as an insurance salesman."

"It doesn't matter what you do as long as you do it well. Insurance salesmen can have perfectly wonderful lives."

"I wouldn't want to be one."

"You'd be solvent."

"I'm a teacher. I'm solvent."

"Yes yes. But your life is an endless temptation."

"And what about an insurance salesman? Isn't every customer a potential temptation?"

"If you say so. I think we're talking at cross-purposes. This young man is trying to find out whether he could live an immoral life and be happy."

"That sounds like W. Somerset Maugham material."

"I can't give you all these objective correlatives. I just want to settle down with someone."

"Don't be too much in a hurry. It will come soon enough. Just enjoy what you have and try to love effectively."

"That's what I am trying to do."

"Well, let us help you. We can be a delightful backdrop. And don't let us cramp your style."

"You're both so wonderful."

"We'll be great friends. You'll see. I have a feeling we'll share a lot over the years."

"Can you see that far ahead?"

"No. But I have feelings."

"You must come down and visit at the college some time soon again."

"I'd like to get a view of your Caravaggio again, if you don't need him."

"You're welcome to him, but I can't guarantee that he would want you."

"We none of us can. That is serendipity. I don't want him. I just want to observe him."

"I'll take you for a pizza and you can observe him all you like."

The sound of a car distracted us. It was Don's jalopy. There he was. My heart began to beat faster and I was almost afraid. Rosie arrived with our lunch on separate trays and we were left alone in the cabin.

"It's been an age," I said, banal.

"It's been an eon," he countered.

We embraced and I felt his arms holding me so tight that I could barely breathe.

"I didn't think I'd ever get back to you. I felt myself drowning everywhere I went. I missed you too much."

"The feeling is mutual."

"Especially on campus. I sat on your stairs and I cried."

"Did you visit Antonio?"

"Once. We just don't hit it off any more. He was pleasant but I could tell. He missed you more."

"Did you visit anyone else?"

"No. I couldn't. I passed by Helmut and Elizabeth's. They're off to Europe for the summer and they sent you their best."

"I'll call them."

"We can't stay here too long. We'll have to make plans."

"That's why I asked you up here. Just for that."

"Let's wait a day before we do. Let's just settle down to being together."

We ate Rosie's hand-me-down food and felt just right.

"Aren't they nice?" I asked.

"You're lucky. People like you. They'd do anything to be on your best side."

"Because I care about people."

"Is that the secret?"

"I guess so. Not everybody likes me."

"Enough do. If you had any more people on your list, you wouldn't have time to work."

"I often don't."

"I want you to know that I love you. I love you with all my heart."

"Why are you saying that?"

"Because I haven't behaved as if I have in quite a while. I tried to see what it would be like to give you up. I played a game with myself. I'm so ashamed."

"Part of you wants to give me up, Don, I know. You have to decide what part wants to keep me. You have to pull all the sides together. If you want me, I'm yours."

"There are too many problems with it."

"Not if you are sure of who you are."

"I made a promise to my parents that I would try to live their lives for a little while. I have a job in Hartford at an insurance company and I start in a month. I promised them."

"But why?"

"I owe them that."

"Well, if you do, so what? You can still have a life of your own. You have evenings and weekends, don't you?"

"No."

"And why not?"

"Because if I do that life, I cannot allow distractions. They'll kill everything. I won't be able to stick with it."

"Suit yourself. Then what does it mean that you love me?"

"Love is impossible. Love is what we want. Life is what we don't want."

"That's maddening. I don't see love or life that way."

"You're free and I'm shackled."

"I'll free you."

"I wish you could."

"I'm going to take you to Paris and we're going to look at another way of living."

"I can't afford it."

"I told you I would take care of that."

"But how will I ever pay you back."

"By loving me."

He held me tight and began to cry. He cried until he shook.

"Please, Don. Don't hurt so."

"Make the plans. Get the tickets. Can we leave soon? I'll allow it for a week. Then I better get back."

"I'll arrange it."

He ate his food as if he hadn't eaten in weeks. Then he threw off his clothes and climbed into the bed. He was asleep within minutes. I walked outside and looked at the sky. The moon was coming up. It was a sliver of a moon. I tried to be happy. Paris might make the miracle needed. We would be far away enough to get a perspective. We would see what it was like to walk the Paris streets and imbibe that atmosphere.

I walked back to the cabin. Don had awakened and thought he had lost me. He extended his arms to me. I fell into them.

"Don't ever leave me, sweetheart."

We held each other like two lost children. I was as bereft as he. I pointed to the sliver of a moon which could be seen through the window.

"That's our moon. It will guide us."

"I'd like to paint it."

"I'll ask Rosie to lend you a canvas."

"I brought a little one, just in case. I only need a place to do it... and an easel."

"You'll have it. I've been posing for her. She's doing a great canvas of three of me. It seems I have multiple personalities."

"I'm the one who has those."

"I'll tell her to paint you."

"Oh, no, you're the subject. You're the star."

"I'm just the witness."

"We're all witnesses."

"Some time we just have to settle down and just be."

"I'm trying."

"I'll try with you."

"Hold me and never let me go."

"You're a crazy mixed-up nut."

"I told you so."

We laughed until we fell asleep. The moon was our witness.

Chapter Thirty-One

"Paris in the spring, tra la tra la…"

"It feels like spring, doesn't it? The most perfect time to be in Paris."

We were walking along the Seine. At one point, in the *Septième*, we crossed the Pont Royal, one of the loveliest bridges and looked down into the moonlit waters.

"Now there's a view." Don was properly impressed.

"One of the most beautiful in the world."

"It's one of the few places that look like a postcard."

"I never thought of that."

"I wonder why it gets so depressing here."

"You've noticed that, too."

"Sometimes I feel as if the rest of the world's troubles started here."

"They probably did. Tolstoy called Paris 'the tomb of the world. *Le tombeau du monde*'."

"He wasn't far from wrong."

"But it's also ecstatically beautiful, don't you think."

"It needs work."

"What do you think it needs?"

"It needs to be cleaned up. The monuments are black."

"Perhaps one day, when there's more money, they'll have a clean-up."

"Then I'll be back."

"I hope they clean it up for you."

It was late in the evening and we had been walking for hours. It took about two hours to cross Paris in any direction and we had criss-crossed as the mood took us. I had a certain delightful old restaurant in mind for a late meal.

"Where are you taking us?"

"There's method to my madness."

"I always knew that."

"Are you hungry?"

"Of course. But I want to be very hungry so I can appreciate it all."

"Good. There's an old-fashioned place about a half hour away and if we're lucky, we can sit outside along the Seine."

"What neighborhood?"

"The Bastille. I often think about this little place and how to find it. It's on an old Quai. Quai de l'Hôtel de Ville."

"What will we eat?"

It was our first evening and Don had refused to go to anything too fancy. I would have liked a three star restaurant or at least a one star but he vetoed all that. He wanted a tiny little place. Fortunately, I knew them, too.

"You'd probably like some pizza, wouldn't you?"

"I wouldn't say no."

"Well, pizzas here are just not too good. You wouldn't go out for French food in Meedletown and expect to get the real thing."

We soon arrived at our destination. The Trumilou was a nice little honkey tonk. The owners, M. et Mme Rouby and their frumpy dog, Soubise, presided, he at the bar and she over the restaurant. They remembered me and embraced me as if I were an old friend. I introduced Don to them and we had a few apéritifs. By the time we sat down at an outdoor table, the restaurant was way past its evening prime.

Don was wild-eyed and just a little high. I had my usual favorites, half a cold langoustine with mayonnaise and an old-fashioned stew with potatoes. Don opted for a pâté with lots of baguettes and mayonnaise and then a crusty old veal cutlet and noodles. We added a bottle of vin rosé to the proceedings. We stopped talking and ate in silence, the way old married couples do. I allowed Don to face out and have the feeling of being in the old city. I contemplated him and kept wondering what he was thinking.

"I'm glad we did this. I'm thinking I'd like to live here."

"A while back I thought you just wanted to get out."

"Both. I have this wonderful sense of discovery. I think of all the painters who lived here and the expatriates and I feel all the heaviness of the past. Then I think there's always a new life to create here, no matter how ancient it looks or feels. And I think that you went to school here and all that culture you teach came from here and I'm in awe."

"You'd love to travel all over Europe."

"I can take it in small doses. I'm not very good at large ones."

"This is only your first night."

"I know but I've already absorbed enough for a lifetime."

"You're not a real tourist."

"No. I just need to smell the place and exist in it. I don't even want to know very much about it."

"You're a small town boy."

"That's right."

"We can leave Paris for a day and try a small town."

"Maybe. This has a feel of a small town compared with New York."

"How do you know?"

"I know from your descriptions of New York."

The conversation ebbed and flowed like a tide. The more we drank, the more it seemed superfluous. Couples walked by on the quai and it was like an obbligato to our experience. The Rouby's floppy dog, Soubise, came by and decided he liked us. He sat down next to me. I patted him and his tail responded. It made me feel as if I could accept all the negativity and the tentativity. It helped me not to feel afraid. After the food, the Roubys offered us a digestif and it was the crowning end of all lucidity. I introduced Don to a Poire Williams, one of the joys of my drinking days. He didn't disagree. We finished everything. I insisted on us having dessert and coffee, which would make it possible to get back to our hotel without a cab.

We waved goodbye to our benefactors and Don insisted on walking along the quais, down by the water. This was something I had never done, it seemed too dangerous. But together it wouldn't be. We came on hobo after hobo and couple after couple, some making love in the shadows. Don would stop every once in a while, take me in his arms and kiss me passionately.

"Now I like Paris."

"Only now?"

"Especially now."

We were hailed by several prostitutes. All this titillated him.

"*Viens, chéri. Je ferai de bonnes petites choses.*"

He seemed as if he would like to go off with them and I was ready to take his arms and run. After a while, we surfaced above the quais again and crossed to the south bank once more. We passed by a *pissoir* and Don made a big to-do about entering one. We stood in separate stations.

Don would peak over at me and I realized he had no intention of peeing. His hand came over to me and took my cock in it. I was almost annoyed but he wanted me to do the same. The other station was filled, as well, and I hardly knew what he might be doing there. He had finally found the Paris that amused him. I finally got out and waited for him.

"Killjoy."

"Go on back if that's what interests you. I'll wait for you right here on the bench. Don't let me cramp your style."

He actually did go back but seemed to tire of the sport if I was not directly with him. That relieved me. It headed us in the right direction of the hotel. I saw that he was getting tired. He finally embraced me round my waist and we walked back like the two brothers that we were. Our hotel had a magnificent façade and the sign on the door stated that both Wagner and Oscar Wilde had spent significant moments there. Don was duly impressed.

"One day they'll have a sign on the house on Oak Street saying that we had once lived there. Or at least you did."

I laughed.

"I really doubt that. There's no sense of history where we come from. It could happen on campus but not in town."

I had wanted a friendly and semi-posh hotel. They had given me a lovely room with a terrace on the front, facing the water. The bed faced a credenza with a magnificent mirror. Don sat there and was reluctant to go to sleep. He wasn't sure what he wanted to do to end his first Parisian twenty-four hours. I would have been glad to call it a day. Dinner was heavy and so was my head.

"Tell me a story."

"A bedtime story?"

"Something I can remember."

"Fine. I was here alone one summer. It was hard for me to go everywhere alone but I didn't have anybody to share it with."

"Sounds promising."

"I was fascinated with *pissoirs*, too. I went into one and met a worker who was building something in the area. We made contact and he made a rendez-vous at my hotel with me. First he went home and dressed up properly in a suit and came back. He understood that the concierge wouldn't allow just anybody to enter the hotel. He came up to my room and we made love. He was an older man, maybe forty-five and infinitely careful in his lovemaking. When we were finished, I was so happy that I asked him to come back the next day or whenever. He told me that he couldn't do that because he didn't live alone but that he wanted to talk to me very seriously because I seemed like a very nice young man and he wanted to say something special to me."

"Don't I ever?"

"Sometimes. But I need to hear something very important from you."

"I'm glad you told me that."

"Well, what did he say?"

Don was needful of a modern Arabian Nights. If I had a story to tell him, he might linger a hundred nights. But he was always in danger of needing to escape.

"He, too, saw there was a mirror in front of the bed. He pulled me up naked so that I could see myself in the mirror. He stood in back of me, holding me up by the waist. It was exhilarating."

"What did he say?"

"He told me I was a very nice boy and that I should always live a good life and appreciate myself, that I should not let people take advantage of me and to know that I was very, very special."

"Were you self-effacing?"

"Perhaps. You know that we all know everything there is to know about other people when we make love to them. He must have sensed that I wasn't my own man."

"A little like me."

"No, Don. You know exactly what you want."

"That's what you say. I just can't take cues. I'm always searching for cues."

"I'm amazed."

Don pulled me up on our bed into the position I had described. He had his hands around my waist and I played myself as a younger man yet again.

"You're a very sweet, wonderful, special man. You must always realize that is you. You must never doubt yourself. You must see that you are the best."

"I'm the one who should be playing this for you. You're the younger man."

"Yes, but you're the special man. Anyway, it doesn't matter what position we're in. As long as the truth is told. And the truth is that you're very wonderful and very special. You are my hero. And the only thing I wonder about is whether I'm good enough for you, whether I could ever live up to what you need and want. I'll try but I'm not very sure I can do it."

We kept the position for an eternity. Then we slumped down on the bed and fell asleep in each other's arms. The first rays of the sun came up as we were falling asleep. Paris was already memorable. It might not be fulfilling but it certainly was memorable.

Chapter Thirty-Two

We had memorable hangovers and found that the coffee we were served hardly took care of them. We dressed and went out for a second round in a nearby café. Neither of us were cheerful. It was a gray day, typically Parisian and the clouds in the high and brilliant sky were suggestively downcast.

"It's getting more and more tomblike. It looks like rain."

"It rains a lot in Paris."

"Well, we had one perfect day and one eventful evening. I feel as if I've seen it all."

"We got a lot in."

We returned to the hotel lobby to get our things ready for another eventful day. The boy at the desk said there was a message for Don. I couldn't imagine his family pursuing him even here. He called back and it took about another half hour for the communication to take place. We sat gloomily in the hotel bar and had yet another round of coffees.

"Why do you think they called?"

"They probably want to know the weather."

"Do you think they want to disrupt our good time?"

"I wouldn't put it past my mother."

"Why does she pursue you so? What did you do to deserve this?"

"I hoped you'd never ask me."

"I thought you might blurt it out sometime this week but it wasn't first on my agenda."

"Well, this might be the best time. Once you hear about it you'll be glad to disrupt our good time, as well."

"Don, please. I'm only interested in your good time. And your happiness."

"Well, the truth is that I'm a fugitive."

"What do you mean?"

"I was caught doing something very wrong in high school."

"What was it?"

"I was always curious about sex. And it couldn't happen fast enough for me."

"Did you rape your sister?" I asked coquettishly.

"No, but I did force a girl at school to do it. And she had me reported."

"Were you punished?"

"No, I got off because my family had influence but they don't trust me. They think I might turn into somebody with no proper morals."

"What do you have to do to convince them?"

"I have to live in the straight and narrow path. And I'm not sure I could ever do that. Sex is too tempting for me. I always want more and more. You know that."

"It's one of your most endearing traits."

"Not to my family. I never had good judgment as to who to get it from."

"Thank you very much."

"You're the living exception, but you know how I behaved with Antonio. And last night in the *pissoir*. I'm not to be trusted."

"And so you want to punish yourself."

"No. I want to be decent and live the right kind of life. And I don't know how I'm going to do it. But I've brought too much down on my parents, already. I have to straighten up and fly right."

"You have to be happy, first."

"No, I have to be moral first."

"You've been brainwashed."

"I owe them something better than I've given them."

"They don't care about you. They only care about themselves."

"I want them to be proud of me."

"And in the process you don't care whether you go down the drain."

"I'll manage. I'll get there. I'll learn to live a good life. They gave me the possibility of college. I didn't let them down. And I won't let them down now. I'm going to take a bourgeois job and make them proud of me."

"And then you'll get married, have two point four children and prove that you're a decent American. How hideous."

"Who knows? That may be the way for me to be happy. This wild life doesn't suit me, either."

"Then why do you hold on to me?"

"Because I love you."

"Doesn't that mean anything?"

"Yes. But they wouldn't approve of it."

"That's the story. You're a prisoner of the bourgeois life."

"It's better than being a sexual deviant."

"I'm not so sure. One can live a good life in any style."

"That's desirable."

"Well, when you make up your mind, you'll let me know."

"I intend to take this job in Hartford and be totally good for one year. If it works for me, I'll keep it. If not, I'll be back."

"Just hope that I'll still be waiting. Knowing me, I probably will."

The doorman came to call Don. He got up like a condemned prisoner and went to find out his fate. I sat there toying with my butter and trying to still my fast beating heart. Yet I still sipped my coffee.

When he returned, it was written on his face.

"Tell me."

"That was my mother. My grandmother died. They want me back for the funeral. I have to leave."

"When?"

"I have to be there in two days, at least."

"Were you close to your grandmother?"

"Yes and no. But my mother wants it."

"And her wish is your command."

"I would say."

"I'll have to make the arrangements."

"I'll pay you back whatever it costs."

"They ought to pay your flight."

"I forgot to ask."

"They must be very upset."

"I think so."

"What a splendid way to snatch you back from the jaws of iniquity. Maybe they made it up."

"You're being unfair."

"Maybe yes and maybe no."

A few hours later we were out at Orly. Don was pale and silent. I followed suit.

"Twenty-four hours in Paris."

"That's what we were allotted."

"But they're a memory."

"They certainly are."

As places were called, we walked up to the entrance together. He turned and embraced me passionately in front of everyone. There were tears in his eyes. "I promise we'll come back here one day together. I'll be in touch. Very soon."

"Take good care of yourself."

"I'll try. And remember. You're very special. I'll love you as long as I live."

"Even if you put me out of your life."

"Don't be cruel."

"Only to be kind."

Now it was my turn to cry. I was dry as dust. Brokenhearted. I returned to the hotel by cab. I didn't know what to do. I wasn't to meet Peter for another ten days in Rome, if that worked out. I started walking all over Paris, retracing our steps. I had to use my umbrella several times as the familiar Paris drizzle commandeered the atmosphere. When I returned to my hotel room, our hotel room, I was bereft.

Suddenly, I thought of calling Anne. I would call the dear soul and pour out my heart to her, if she was there in New York.

To my utter surprise, I got her right away.

"Sweetheart, how lovely."

I told her what had happened.

"Worse luck. But what if he had ruined the rest of your stay with his foul behavior and moods?"

"What shall I do? I have most of the work here. I can't bear it by myself."

"I'll fly right over, my dear. My parents have been absolutely wonderful to me now that I am going to be married. I can make an excuse to my husband and actually do well buying some of my trousseau right here. You'll help me to pick out my wedding dress. That will be perfect. I'll stay with you at your hotel. You won't lose any money and we'll economize together."

"I love you."

"If I could believe that, I'd jilt my husband and spend the rest of my life with you. You're the one I always wanted, you dear sweet boy."

"If your marriage doesn't work out, you can claim me."

"It better work out. I'm three months pregnant, already. It's somewhat of a shotgun marriage. He has to do it and I think he made me pregnant purposely so that I would marry him."

"Don't you want to?"

"Not particularly. I didn't want to be a faculty wife. But you see, it's so respectable. My parents were utterly delighted. Their bohemian daughter is going to be a faculty wife."

"Can you stand it?"

"I guess I can, for a while. I want to have my children young, before I become an international slut all over again."

"Well, maybe you won't have to."

"We'll discuss it."

"Let me know when you're arriving."

"I'll take a cab from the airport. Just be there."

"Anne, you'll never know how happy you've made me."

"It's *pari-mutuel*, as my mother says."

"I'll be waiting."

"Much love."

We hung up and for the first time, the loss of Don was

bearable. I thought I would die and now I would probably survive. Life was full of surprises. Now I could even bear not meeting Peter in Rome. I would play it by ear.

Chapter Thirty-Three

Anne sat having her postprandial cigarette. We were in one of those wonderful old restaurants which her parents loved so much. The chairs were all upholstered in tapestries of the time of Watteau.

"I'm so glad we have this time together. I wanted to get away and have time to think."

"You saved me."

"You were too generous to Don."

"Not really. He wanted to give himself to me and he just didn't have the ability to do so. He's a victim of his family."

"We're all victims if we allow ourselves to be."

"You have to be lucky not to be a victim."

"You're right. It takes a lot of gumption."

"But you're not the victim type."

"No. But if I allow myself to become a faculty wife, I might get that way soon."

"Then why are you allowing yourself to do it?"

"I'm three months pregnant and I want my child to grow up knowing his father. That's sacred to me."

"I understand that."

"Still, if his father abuses me, the situation will change."

"In what way could he abuse you?"

"He wants his own way all the time. He's passionate and controlling. He wishes me to obey him in all things."

"That doesn't sound like you."

"You're right. I can't allow myself to be controlled full time. A little bit goes a long way."

"If you run into great difficulties, I'll help you."

"I'm counting on that. I want you at the wedding and at the divorce, whenever that occurs."

"Perhaps it won't. Try and stick with it."

"It's one way to calm my parents and get their support. It has a lot of advantages. Still, I won't be in New York. And that's not a plus for me."

"Yale is a fine place. It has its own advantages."

"I don't mind a house but I certainly don't want to be stuck in New Haven."

"Children grow up quickly and you have the means to travel."

"I know. I'm being a bit defensive. One step at a time."

"Meanwhile, we can enjoy Paris together and plan for the future. I want to pick up some drop-dead clothes."

"Ready, set, go."

We spent the afternoon shopping wildly and almost indiscriminately. The only thing that made me jealous were the items from Charvet. But Anne made me feel like a member of the wedding by buying me a few of the finest silk ties and kerchiefs. I would treasure them always. She outfitted herself in blue and white silks and satins. By the time we finished our first day of acquiring, we were totally exhausted. Jet lag was upon us. We cabbed back to the hotel and took occupancy in the salon. Anne sat on the gorgeous blue divan which Don and I had never touched. I looked out the terrace window to imbibe the late afternoon Paris atmosphere. I even meditated what it would be like to be her lover and seduce her in these luscious circumstances. I was planning to sit by her on the couch and take her in my arms. What would she do?

As I came towards her, wondering how I could make my first crucial move, the phone rang.

It was Peter.

"Peter, how are you? What a nice surprise. I was hoping you'd call. Will I have the pleasure of your company? Splendid. I suggest you book directly for Rome. Then take a cab from the airport into town, to the Croce di Malta, off Piazza di Spagna. S–p–a–g–n–a. Yes, and C–r–o–c–e. Not crotche, you idiot. I can take a joke. Yes, I can. Well, I'll be there awaiting your arrival, you can be sure. And then we'll have a fine week. Yes, you can see Rome in a week. Rome and even a villa. I'll show it all to you. If you have any questions, I'll be here for the rest of this week. I'm spending it with a lovely lady whose wedding I'll be attending in New York shortly after. Now don't be jealous. It is a lady, of that you can be sure. Take good care of yourself. And dress lightly. It's summertime. It gets very hot in Rome. Now that's enough."

Anne took it all in and stared at me.

"I can see why you weren't entirely devastated by the loss of Don in Paris."

"That's not true. Only you saved me. Peter couldn't. He's just a fantastic fling I am settling next week."

"Your life is even more interesting than mine, I can see."

"Not really. I just have to learn how to end things. There's no future in any of this. Dear old Peter is having a fling with the boys before he, too, enters married life."

"Maybe it's all too premature."

"All my loves will marry other people while I go on to older age lonelier and wiser."

"Don't make me cry."

"I'm not. I'm just afraid nobody will ever stay with me."

"Perhaps you don't really ask loudly enough. You could have had me."

"I may yet claim you down the line."

"That's what I'm hoping."

"Meanwhile, you have to be a good faculty wife, *n'est-ce pas?*"

"I'll try. Now I have to take a nap and then you'll surprise me with dinner, I hope, at some quiet little place."

"It will be my pleasure. But you have to be ready by eight or so because dinner will be very late. We have a concert to go to at nine, at the Salle Pleyel."

"Nifty."

I kissed her on the mouth. We played at being husband and wife or fiancé and fiancée. She pressed her lanky body to mine and I felt the beginnings of passion.

Chapter Thirty-Four

The recital featured *Carnaval*.

"What a hoot!"

"I wish you were playing it."

"One day I will."

"I wanted to hear it with you, to see what the variations of interpretation would be like. I doubt I could have listened to it if you weren't here."

"Romantic!"

"It's a sacred moment."

"You could have listened to it with Don."

"If he had wanted to hear it. One never knew, with him."

"Let's listen."

The pianist played with considerable passion. The fact that he was a man made little difference. So many female pianists play as strongly or more so than men. He played with gossamer swiftness and the piece seemed to go by too fast. Afterwards, it was my only criticism. It didn't give us time to breathe.

We walked along the quais and it took us quite a bit of time to get to the Trumilou. I was even surprised they were still serving. They were the one stable part of my Parisian life. The Roubys greeted me with infinite sweetness and no mention of my previous companion. Soubise loved the presence of Anne just as much. We enjoyed our meal with zest. She, too, loved the langoustine with the unctuous mayonnaise. We didn't eat a great deal because we were so tired.

"So you take all your friends here. What a lovely place. Cuisine bourgeoise. Country cooking here in the heart of Paris."

"With you it seems so natural. So inevitable."

"One day we'll come back here, when we're older and wiser, and remember everything we did when we were young adventurers."

Anne blew her cigarette out towards the Seine and we clinked glasses as we consumed our postprandial digestifs. We walked until we found a cab and were soon in our comfortable quarters.

We lay in bed together, happily ensconced. I held her in my arms.

"I wish I were the father of your child."

"That's so tender of you."

"It would be so natural. That's perhaps what is missing from my life. Sexual expression isn't the be all and end all of existence."

"Isn't it?"

"No. Tenderness, love, peace, contentment, all the subtleties of life. These are what count."

"You're right, I suppose. Sexual ecstasy is good for a time. But it deteriorates eventually. And if there's nothing to replace it with, then there is nothing but a world of indifference."

We kissed tenderly and she was asleep before I could evaluate the meaning of the kiss. I lay next to her for the longest time, unable to sleep, and then wondering whether Don was surviving. Why did Anne make me think of Don? We three were inextricably joined somewhere. If I were to get over him, it would only be with her. Inevitably with her. And get over him I knew I must. It was so strong in me that I almost dreaded going to Rome for an adventure. I'd had so many adventures. Peter would have to work very hard to make this one valid. And before that, Anne and I would have to exhaust Paris together. Decidedly, Paris was beginning to be difficult to take. It always had this effect on me of total exhaustion. Too much happened too quickly. I held Anne in my arms, hard and fast. She was so deep in her slumbers that she never awoke. I would have to tell her about my thoughts. How receptive would she be?

Chapter Thirty-Five

We left our hotel and walked into the bright, humid sunlight of the Via Borgognona and to Piazza di Spagna. This was the hub of Rome and contained a felt life experience beyond anything else I had known. Roma was a gorgeous jungle full of life and every step of it was like living through history. Peter marched next to me with his customary vigor. He had been particularly subdued since he arrived. Was it jetlag, was it the fact that we were far from anything he had ever known before... He even forgot to utter his usual refrain: "Hi teach."

One of the major excitements of Rome was the sudden arrival at a new vista. Here, in the approximate center of the Piazza, one came on the fashionable via Condotti, full of *maisons de couture*, the lovely fountain in the middle and then the drama of it all: the hundreds of steps leading up to the Villa Borghese. Peter was spellbound as we stood gaping up the steps.

"We won't climb to the top yet, though a friend of mine showed me a foolproof way to get to the top without losing breath control. One inhaled on the first step, then exhaled on the second and alternated that way smoothly to the top. Otherwise, if you keep going, you're liable to get winded."

"Not me. But I believe you."

"Are you hungry?"

"Sure."

"Right here there's an old Roman establishment where they speak English. It's Babington's Tea Room. You have to have breakfast there once. It's not that the food is so great, but the ambiance is."

We entered and sat down. I felt that Peter would be happier if they spoke his language. On the other side of the Piazza was Keats's house and we would see that later. We both ordered French toast which turned out to be embellished zwieback.

"I see what you mean. Even Middletown wouldn't sell you something like this. But still it's fun. I like a real breakfast."

We were working away on our zwieback when a couple of what were surely businessmen walked in and took the next table. One of the gentlemen, of Chinese descent, was in a fury. He spoke so audibly that we didn't miss a word of his diatribe. He had wanted to visit Pompeii.

Peter looked at me and wished he could do the same. "I hear it's a gas."

I shushed him so that we could hear the rest of the complaint. He had been booked by an Italian company called CIT, a company of international transit. CIT was pronounced like the 'cheat' that it surely was. We were already chuckling. The man was so put out that he even broadcast his traveler's lament to the tables nearby. They had booked him on an airplane going to Bombay. It was when he arrived in Cairo that he was aware that he had been misunderstood. Pompeii, Bombay, surely one of the most delightful traveler's stories ever told.

"I'm sure glad I have you next to me. I bet I would have fallen into that trap, as well. You've got to be clever over here or you'll get royally ripped off."

"Even if you are clever and trilingual, it all depends on dumb luck. More people get mugged here than anywhere else in the world."

"Then why do you like being here?"

"It's the most exciting city in the world. Don't you enjoy looking at it?"

"I'll enjoy it when I wake up. This French toast is going to make me want to sleep even more."

"Do you wish you were back in Middletown?"

"No. But I'm trying to get my bearings."

"I thought it would be easier to talk to each other in strange surroundings. They bring out the authenticity in everyone."

"I keep forgetting where we are. I keep thinking we'll move out of one place and find ourselves on campus again. But meanwhile, it's an adventure and I wanted that adventure with you."

"What shall we do to keep you amused?"

"I put myself in your hands. You decide. We're doing pretty well already."

"Good. After this I'm going to walk you through one of the prettiest parts of Rome, the Villa Borghese. It has the most beautiful trees and walkways and somewhere in the middle there is the wonderful Museo Borghese where you'll see some of the sexiest paintings on earth, the early Caravaggios."

"I remember you telling us that Roma was a festival of Caravaggios. He certainly knew how to paint sexy men. I wonder if he liked them."

"He certainly did. He used to pick up all the subjects of his paintings, men as well as women, and he dared to use them as models for his paintings, in which there were saints as well as sinners. If he hadn't been such a great painter, he might have spent his life in prison. He was arrested quite a few times and was somewhat of a bully and a murderer."

"One day you ought to write his life story."

"His death was the most dramatic tale of all. He was a fugitive from the law. He was trying to escape and take with him his entire treasure of paintings, those he had held on to. He had them placed on a boat. But he arrived too late to capture the boat and it left without him. He started running along the coast line and he ran along the coast until he went mad and contracted some disease like malaria and he died brokenhearted."

"What happened to the paintings?"

"They found their ways into museums, mostly, and there they still are. But his life was one of the most tragic ever recorded. He was ugly and mean and a genius."

"The greats never had an easy time of it, did they?"

"That's why it's better to live the good life and travel to see the work of the greats."

"That's what I intend to do."

We paid, nodded to the furious Chinese businessman and walked up the stairs, huffing and puffing in the sharp light of day. Once we got up to the Villa Borghese, we sat down on lovely benches and watched the world go by.

Peter offered me his tiny little silver thermos, filled with vodka. I didn't refuse and we imbibed a little just to be a tiny bit high while we took in the splendors of Rome. I made sure to bring him to the fountain of Moses, my favorite little place there. We took photos of each other in front of it. Moses in the bullrushes. Then we looked long and hard down to the magnificent Piazza del Popolo.

"There are great Caravaggios in the church down there. We'll visit them if we have time."

"What do we do when we get hungry again? I'm ready to wolf down Rome."

"We'll go have pasta somewhere. There are no bad restaurants in this country. It's the best food in the world."

"We'll have a great meal and then we'll go back to the hotel and have a nap. I want you for dessert."

"That's the first indication to me that my Peter is with me."

"I've been living a different life. I've spent the last week with Susie and her parents. It's enough to kill sex forever."

"Why?"

"It's oh so proper. And it's really nice. They're very fine people. And they stand for something at their university and in the community. They are good people, I tell you."

"Are you tired of them already?"

"Not exactly. They give me a sense of what I might become if I was respectable. They make me feel like I could grow up."

"Then why did you come to Rome?"

"When I'm with them, I'm not sure. But when I'm with you, I get to feeling like life is a socko adventure and that I'm living it to the hilt. Then all I want to do is come."

"You mean that if you get married and live a respectable life, you'll stop making love."

"You know, that seems to be it. I don't think about sex when I'm respectable. It's another world. What turns me on is learning."

"But you'll be living near a university."

"I guess it's not the university. Or maybe there are sexy universities and non-sexy ones."

"I think I know what you mean."

"Do you? Then explain it to me."

"I think you're turned on by professors."

"You're the first one who ever turned me on."

"What about professor's wives?"

"I doubt it. I think I'm really potentially totally gay. Women are to be respected, revered, the mothers of your children."

"What if a man could have children?"

"That would kill it for me."

"Well, I'm certainly glad it isn't possible."

"I think I'm on my way to disgusting you."

"Not at all, Peter. In a way, I'm relieved. I didn't want to have to rescue you from an unhappy marriage. Now I know you're on your way to having one."

"Happy or unhappy?"

"That's for you to figure out. I think you're potentially the typical guilty American man."

"Guilty of what."

"Guilty of wanting to live an exciting life."

"Are you going to spend your life living that life?"

"I certainly hope so."

"Aren't you ever going to settle down?"

"What do you mean by that?"

"Don't you want to leave a name behind you?"

"Certainly, but does that have to mean marriage and children?"

"Who will you leave your worldly goods to? Who will carry on your name?"

"I don't know."

"Well, think about it. One day you'll be tired of sleeping around."

"This was not my idea, Peter. It was yours."

"I know. I feel a little guilty. I feel like I corrupted you."

"Don't have any illusions. It happened a long time ago."

"Yeah. But the sex we've had is the greatest. You'll never find anything like that again."

"Will you?"

"Never."

"So?"

"That brings me back to my original thought. I think we should meet for one week a year and go on vacations together. Then we could have that memory for the rest of our lives."

"What will you do if one of us leaves this world before the other?"

"I don't want to think about that. I just want to know that you and I are a sure thing forever. If I know that, I can go ahead and marry Susie and live that life and be content."

"What if I refuse?"

"Hear me out. You can't refuse. We happened. What happened to us happened. So that was meant to be. All we have to do is calm it down and live good lives."

"What if our vacations don't coincide?"

"You're being an asshole. We'll make them coincide."

"What if Susie has a baby on our vacation moment?"

"Then we'll reschedule. You're just trying to make me feel bad."

"No. I'm trying to save myself."

"Let's eat."

We walked and walked and finally got out of the villa, forgetting Caravaggios and just about reaching a little trattoria before the lunch hour was officially over. Peter was fascinated with the tomatoes in the salad.

"Red and green and still so delicious. These Italians really have it made."

By the time we got back to our hotel, we were exhausted.

Peter got into bed, forgetting to take off his clothes.

"Are you that tired?"

"Yeah. Let's make love when we wake up."

He was snoring in half a second. It was a joy to see him in this way, a huge bit of Americana exhausted by a new culture. He would never get used to Rome. He would never want to go abroad for a vacation. He would probably become old before his time. That is, if he stopped exercising, which it seemed might happen. All that pulchritude would turn to fat.

When he awoke, he went into the john and relieved himself. I had not slept at all. I was too taken with all my subjects of contemplation. Peter came into the room naked, still magnificent, still a fine specimen of manhood. His eternal penis was still as eternal in the eternal city. When pleasure was upon him, he wished to be instantly pleasured. He wanted to tuck his plaything into anywhere that would satisfy it. He needed no foreplay. He needed play.

"Hurry. I'm going to come."

"Don't you want to make love?"

"Next time. I just want to come. If you don't help me, I'll come anyway."

Which is what he did, moaning with pleasure for a good five minutes.

"You sound like a woman having an orgasm."

"Sometimes I think I would have been a terrific cunt. I love to moan when I have sex. But I can't do that with a woman. Only with a man."

"Why not?"

"It's like I don't want them to know what pleasure it gives me. You give me that pleasure."

"But I didn't do anything."

"You didn't need to. I'm with you. That's enough."

"You're amazing."

"Don't you want to come? I'll get excited working on you."

Which he did. We both had a rousing orgasm and then drank some more from his snifter.

"I think I could get to like your Rome."

"If you don't have to see too much of it."

"That's right. Just a few minutes here and there. The rest of the time, I want to be intimate with you. You do it to me, baby."

We both showered again and then went out to a local bar for a fortifying drink. Then I walked him over to one of my favorite places in Rome. It was a sixth-century church, Santa Cecilia, which contained within it one of the great statuettes of the ancient world. It was a baroque face with a huge sliver of a mouth. It was called La Boca della Verità, the Mouth of Truth, and the superstition which went with it was that if you placed your hand in it and lied, you would be punished. In ancient times, you might be bitten by a tarantula.

"Now place your hand in the mouth of truth. I want to take a picture of you doing that."

"Why?"

"It's a wonderful memory. And if you are lying about caring about me, I want to know."

"I'm not lying."

"Good."

"I want the same from you. You place your hand in and I'll take a picture. Turnabout is fair play."

"Very well."

"That way I can tell whether or not you're worth all my devotion."

"I think I'm worth it."

We did the deed and ended up having a great laugh over it. We were both relieved we hadn't been bitten. We then kept walking and were soon at another major thoroughfare of beauteous Roma, the Via Veneto. We had yet another drink and then went to one of the posh restaurants nearby. Piccolo Mondo was just the ticket. We ate up a storm and even had a mighty dessert. Peter was beginning to enjoy himself royally.

"You know, this day just goes on and on and on and it's wonderful."

"I wanted to share this with you. There's a Roman emperor hidden somewhere in you and that guilty American just doesn't relate to it."

"You see, you were always my teach."

After dinner, we went back to the Veneto and sat at a café, imbibing grappas and punctuating them with much needed espressi.

"It's the best coffee in the world."

"Why can't we get such coffee?"

"It's not the coffee, it's the water."

"But we have great water and the water in Europe is so dangerous, I hear you have to drink mineral water everywhere just to avoid the runs."

"The water is fabulous here, and it's purified in the coffee."

"Well, that's a good reason to come back."

A distinguished group of people sat down at the next table. In the center of the group was a most impressive looking woman with a deep, resonant voice. Her meaningful eyes were shadowed in black and she had a commanding laugh.

"Now there's a great looking broad."

"I know who she is," I suddenly realized.

"She looks like a movie star."

"She is. Movies and stage. Her name is Anna Magnani."

"I think I've heard that name."

"She's known the world over. When we meet at home, we can see some of her old movies."

"She kind of looks like she's had it."

"She always looked like that."

"These famous people lead terrible lives."

"Unfortunately. They're too sensitive. Life takes a toll on them."

"It takes a toll on us, too. At least they are famous."

"Do you like famous people, Peter?"

"That sounds like a trap."

"Whatever for?"

"I don't care about famous people, but if they're around, why not look at them?"

"That's right. They might have a story to tell."

"We all have a story to tell. One day, on one of our annual meetings, we might have a story to tell."

"I'm sure we will."

"I want to save up all my fame for you. I'll sit there and be proud that I knew my teach."

"What did you say? That you blew your peach?"

I was feeling silly and it was the only answer to this experience. I could not allow it to disintegrate into a tragedy the way Don's Parisian visit had. Not all relationships had to end badly. Some of them could be amusing and fulfilling and fun, as well. I would try to retain Peter as a good part of my life, a warm, decent, orgiastic pleasurable part of my life. It could be done simply because we wouldn't be spending that much time together. If we met once a year, it would be a miracle, but we might have occasional travels together and it could keep us sane.

Anna Magnani and company drifted down the Via Veneto and I would never forget the sound of their lovely voices. I would romanticize that forever. Peter and I paid the piper and then walked home in the Roman night. By the time we reached the Piazza di Spagna, there were few people left. A few horses and carriages still stood at attention, waiting to snag some late night romantics. Though we were properly exhausted, Peter and I lingered in the piazza before getting back to the hotel room. It had none of the poetry of the hotel in Paris. It was basically a bed, a window and a tiny terrace looking out on the via Borgognona. It had the smell of sex without the drama of love.

Peter poured vodka over my body and licked it off. "You're pretty salty, you know."

"So are you."

"Next time I won't need peanuts."

We both giggled and went on with the orgy. It seemed appropriate. By the time we were finished, dawn had come up. We went out on the terrace and watched a few die-hard stay-ups walking through the streets. We were both high on the experience.

Chapter Thirty-Six

Middletown in August was sweltering for the late summer season. I walked down the streets to my office and felt that I was in some ghost town. Short sojourns in Paris and Rome had somehow changed me completely. I was somewhat cured of Don, excited by Anne, amused, as ever, by Peter. I wished Helmut and Elizabeth were back. They were probably somewhere in Vienna or Budapest. They had sent a sweet, commemorative postcard. Everywhere I walked, I felt the presence of someone with whom I had shared a moment. The office was in great shape. Only in a small town could things remain intact. One never needed to worry. Everything remained the same. I dreaded spending more than a moment in the apartment. It was there that Don was most potently with me. I knew that my sense of bravado would not last long. If any of our strong memories were unleashed, I would surely be in that misery I was saved from in Paris.

All I had to do was to gather my New York wardrobe for the wedding, telephone Anne and make the last arrangements. If I were to feel particularly needful, I could go have a pizza and see what that meant.

As I walked back toward the apartment, a familiar figure was walking toward me. Could it be? But how? It was Beatrice, alone, melancholy, but obviously happy to see me. We embraced strongly and decided to have coffee together.

"Where have you been?"

"I spent a week in Paris and then a week in Rome. Haven't you been away?"

"No. I promised Paul I'd visit him in Hawaii, but I couldn't bring myself to do it."

"Has Aram left?"

"Oh yes, on graduation day. And now I have to pick up the pieces."

"Where are all the people you've been so good to?"

"They're leading their lives."

"How's your son?"

"He's off with his father and his new girlfriend. They're a lot more cheerful than I am."

"And what about Andrew? Didn't he owe you anything?"

"He offered to take me to Europe with him. I couldn't face that."

"But you need a life. You can't just be alone."

"Why not? I've had my life. I'm a mother, I read books, I cook for people and have an occasional affair. What more could I want?"

"A great deal more, which you deserve. I wish I could do something for you."

"You're still young and romantic and you still believe in your affairs."

"One has to."

"Yes, but after a certain moment, the belief ends."

"I know, but still one has to insist there will be more."

"You're amusing. You're such an American."

"Do you really think so? Europeans don't have a monopoly on disbelief, you know."

"Don't worry about me. All I need is a good meal occasionally, a fine conversation and a good read."

"That terrible couple has left, haven't they?"

"Yes. But I was a fool. I thought the book was evil. It wasn't the book at all, it was my last hope that he wouldn't leave me."

"You're better off without him."

"We're all better off without what destroys our lives, but we can't always bring ourselves to be lucid."

"Beatrice, you have to promise me that you will try to pick up the pieces and enjoy your life."

"I promise."

We embraced and I went back, dejected, to the apartment. I put on the Brando record and tears came to my eyes. I phoned Anne, my perpetual antidote.

"Sweetheart. I was just thinking about you."

"How are you?"

"With child. The baby is kicking me."

"Is the wedding going off as planned?"

"If it doesn't, I'm going to lose my reputation."

"What reputation?"

"How was Rome?"

"A hoot. Certainly better than Paris, except for you."

"You're just saying that."

"Do you have any last minute instructions?"

"Yes, bring a few changes of clothes. I want you to meet my parents and go everywhere with us. I want you by my side."

"Won't they object?"

"Of course not. They'll be as charmed by you as my husband is."

"Why do you keep referring to him as your husband?"

"Because he'd never make it as my lover."

"I'll see you tomorrow."

"Good. You can stay with me. I'll be so nervous that I'll need lots of TLC."

"Torrid love calls?"

"I can't wait for you to get here. Don't dawdle."

We wished each other love and there I was, alone again. The phone rang.

"Don, where are you?"

"I'm in Hartford. I'm working."

"Then why did you call?"

"I wanted to hear your voice."

"You made me promise not to call."

"What's good for the goose."

"I want to see you. Drive down here for the night."

"I can't. I won't. If I do that, I'll quit my job and all my good resolutions will be over."

"How was the funeral?"

"Perfect. It fit my mood."

"How's your family?"

"As ever. They're very proud of me. For the moment."

"Bully for them."

"I love you."

"What does that mean?"

"Whatever you like?"

"How do you like your job?"

"It'll do."

"Do you like working with tables and money?"

"I guess so."

"What did you do with your paintings?"

"I destroyed most of them. They were no good."

"You promised me some."

"I delivered them. You'll find them in your hall closet."

"Thank you."

"I'm a man of my word."

"Anne is getting married this weekend. I'm going to the wedding."

"Wish her well for me."

"We'll be thinking about you."

"What will you do this evening?"

"I think I'll have a pizza, if you won't join me."

"Don't tempt me."

"You remind me of a priest. You've given up living."

"Give Antonio my best regards."

"I'll do that."

"Stop trying to tempt me."

"I just want to see you, you idiot."

"Let me have a better memory of you than I have at this moment."

"Shall I send you a valentine?"

"No. Please don't do that."

"I was just joking."

"Be good. Be patient. One day we'll see each other again."

"Do you expect me to wait forever?"

"No. Live your life as you have to live it. I'm doing that."

"Good. Well then, Don, I wish you all the best. I will always remember you with the greatest fondness. And if you come towards me, I'll knock you down."

I hung up with a thud. I had lost my temper. I had promised not to. He had gone too far. I couldn't bear his miserable meanness. I burst into tears of rage. Perhaps I only wanted to be obeyed. I couldn't bear this stupid farewell. I was in the pain I had resolved not to feel. I couldn't bear this place without him. I would have to get out. Life was too short to suffer two nights in Meedletown. New York would have to absorb me.

I would pack later. I opened the hall closet and saw the ambiguous drawing of the boy-girl. Don had never figured out what he was. He was androgynous in mind and soul. He was a failed rapist. He had the soul of a priest and the nature of a sadist. I would try to hate him as much as possible. He was not civilized. He was brutal. He was my failed lover. He was the reason why I would become the next Beatrice in town. People who cared too much always lost everything. Not caring was the secret of living. Peter had the right idea. Peter would always be hale and hearty because he didn't care enough about anything. That was the secret of success. I knew I was wrong but I wasn't sure in what way or how much. The only answer was to keep living and find out.

I drove over to the pizza place. Antonio was not there. I found out he was on vacation. Everything was perfect. Sour and perfect. Sour and terrible. I allowed my tears to fall into my pizza. Whoever replaced him wasn't even as good at the *métier*. I paid quickly and decided to go home and drink myself into oblivion. When I arrived at the house, I was thunderstruck. Antonio was knocking at my door. Joy spread through every pore. I ran up the stairs, let us in and allowed him to make mad passionate love to me, as if I were his paramour. He was drunk with happiness, as was I. I decided that everything in life was timing. That was the ultimate answer.

"Oh, Antonio, make love to me. Be my savior."

He obliged.

Chapter Thirty-Seven

Anne sat smoking with a vengeance.

"Don't overdo it."

"I hate him."

"That's natural before you get married. You can think of all the reasons why you would never want to do it. All my friends tell me the night before and the hours before are lethal."

"He has no consideration for me. He's an autocrat. He's a tyrant."

"You'll get used to it."

"I never will. I lay bets the marriage will be over in short shrift."

"What about your child needing its father?"

"It can have him."

"Now stop, dear. I didn't know you were so temperamental."

"We show our best sides to our friends."

"We have to have somebody to show our best sides to."

"I'm sorry, dear. You don't deserve this."

"Especially since Don dumped on me even worse."

"What did the bastard do?"

"He called me right after I hung up with you and then said he loved me, but he couldn't see me. I was so angry, I hung up on him."

"You did right."

"Only you and I are any good."

"We're the good ones. Why didn't we end up with each other? We could have made each other happy. We could have. You know that."

"Well, we're in this together."

"Not quite. I wouldn't want you to have to deal with him."

"I didn't mean that. I'm by your side."

"You're my brother."

"I'm the brother you never had and you're the sister I never had."

At this juncture, Anne's mother entered, a very stylish lady, formidable as she had said.

"Mother, I want you to meet my best friend, Roy."

"I've heard so much about you. How do you like my bohemian daughter consenting to become a bourgeois wife?"

"I think it's splendid."

"So do I."

"Well I don't," Anne boasted. "You don't have to marry him, I do."

"I want you to do me a favor, Roy, and control my little girl. She's impossible these days. I wasn't that way when I got married."

"The first time."

"You're rude, my dear. The first time didn't count."

"But this is my first time."

"First and last, my dear, I hope."

"Balls!"

"Please behave in front of your friend. He seems like a very civilized man."

Now her father entered. He was a handsome devil. She obviously loved and feared him. None of her previous behavior was echoed.

We took turns calming Anne and I was rather happy to be a member of the wedding. It kept me from thinking of my own problems. That really was the purpose of friends and relationships: they could keep us from thinking about the worst parts of our love lives. They were the much needed consolation.

Next appeared her professor. There I sat and smiled and hoped I wasn't being noticed too much. We all went to dinner in a very posh place and I kept smiling at pregnant moments. I discussed theater, films, books, French and otherwise, and was amazed at my ability to analyze just about anything that was needed for the conversation. Anne kept smoking and hitting my hand or just holding it under the table. I felt positively conspiratorial.

The next evening, after the wedding at the Waldorf Astoria, I had Anne in tow, dancing with her. She was positively subdued in white organdy.

"You look so beautiful."

"That's my façade."

"Never mind. You are gorgeous."

"I've got to be something."

"Well, you are, and you have to promise to behave for a while."

"You're on my mother's side."

"She wants the best for you."

"You've been brainwashed."

"I hope so."

"Do you believe any of this?"

"I believe it all. It's called the willing suspension of disbelief."

We both started laughing at the top of our lungs and a great many of the guests turned to look at us. At that moment, the rather bourgeois wedding was graced by the *pièce de résistance*. The ceiling opened up and the guests were showered with thousands of pennies as the band played *Pennies from Heaven*. Everyone got on their knees to be able to retrieve the bounty. I found this piece of unspeakable vulgarity perfectly consonant with the occasion. I started humming some of *Carnaval*. It was not easy to do that as counterpoint to the band. Anne stared at me. We were among the few who didn't stoop to conquer the pennies. I sang the Davidsbündler march triumphantly and she finally realized what I was doing. She was divinely happy suddenly.

"I love you. You know how to make me happy."

"That's the great secret of life, isn't it."

We went on dancing for hours and hours. At one point I decided to leave. I walked out into the New York night, exhilarated. Park Avenue was as beautiful as ever. I would leave Meedletown and come here to make my fortune. It was time to grow up. It was time to have a life.